MOUNTAIN MURDER INVESTIGATION

KAREN KIRST

LOVE INSPIRED SUSPENSE

INSPIRATIONAL ROMANCE

LOVE INSPIRED® SUSPENSE
INSPIRATIONAL ROMANCE

ISBN-13: 978-1-335-72303-1

Mountain Murder Investigation

This edition published by arrangement with Harlequin Books S.A.

For questions and comments about the quality of this book, please contact us at CustomerService@Harlequin.com.

Love Inspired
22 Adelaide St. West, 41st Floor
Toronto, Ontario M5H 4E3, Canada
www.LoveInspired.com

Printed in U.S.A.

Recycling programs for this product may not exist in your area.

PLEASE RECYCLE — THIS PRODUCT IS RECYCLABLE

My brethren, count it all joy
when ye fall into divers temptations; Knowing this,
that the trying of your faith worketh patience.
—*James* 1:2–3

To Jacob, Austin and Daniel. I'm blessed to be your mom and grateful for the years we've spent together during our homeschool journey. I'm proud of you.

ONE

Serenity, Tennessee

Mounted Police Officer Raven Hart entered her dark, silent house and instinctively reached for her 9mm. The night-light near the sink window wasn't on as usual. She hadn't touched it, and her roommate, Lindsey, wouldn't be home until late. The stove clock wasn't flashing. Nothing was wrong with the electricity.

She listened for unusual sounds. Her worn-out body longed for a soak in the tub and a full eight hours of sleep. Five was the most she'd managed at once since Aiden's death thirteen months and ten days ago. She gritted her teeth. She had to stop counting the days. Had to stop feeling guilty. Raven had been in Serenity when his car had veered off that Morganton road and plunged into an icy river.

Flicking on the overhead light, her fingers left the holster to whisper over the photo hanging on the fridge. It was a close-up of her and Aiden, taken on the university campus where he'd taught architecture. His face was pressed close to hers, and they were both grinning like fools. Her chest grew tight as she imagined the moments leading to his death.

Trapped. Struggling to escape. To breathe.

Somehow his body had never been found. He had to have gotten free of the car and been swept away by the swift current. The local authorities theorized he'd been pinned underwater by the thick network of vines and roots. Less likely, his body had drifted far downriver and into an isolated cove.

Raven pressed her palm to her forehead, as if she could stop the images those theories created.

Nothing good can be gained by fixating on the circumstances surrounding his passing. Naomi, a widow at church who'd become something of a mentor to Raven, had lost her husband to an unexpected tragedy. Naomi and Raven had spoken many times about grief and moving on from loss. But there was something Naomi didn't know. Something no one did. People might not be so quick to extend compassion if they knew the truth.

Raven unzipped her leather jacket and shrugged it off, the tension in her shoulders radiating into her neck and the base of her skull. A monster headache was brewing. Their mounted police unit's monthly training sessions always took a toll on her. The sights and sounds meant to de-sensitize the horses wreaked havoc on her dys-lexic brain. She had to pour every ounce of her energy into not losing focus and not distracting her equine partner, Thorn.

The floorboards emitted a groaning shift somewhere near the guest bathroom. Raven was used to the sounds her riverside bungalow made—and this wasn't one of them. Her scalp prickled. Various scenarios scrolled through her mind. Sliding her gun from her holster, she inched between the table and stove and paused beside the fridge. A distorted rectangle of light probed the navy-and-white living room, giv-ing her an unobstructed view of the oak boards, muted rug and giant marshmallow ottoman. Be-yond that, she could make out the shapes of her sofa, the built-in bookshelves flanking the fire-place and French doors leading to the backyard and languid river beyond.

Holding her weapon with both hands, she inched around the corner. Another sound greeted her—a footstep and an audible exhale. There, in the juncture between the hallway and bathroom, was the unmistakable hulk of a man. Raven's in-stincts took over.

She rammed into him, knocking him into the

wall. His breath escaped in a whoosh and he stumbled sideways. Picture frames hit the floor and splintered. She swiped her booted leg beneath his feet. He went down and didn't come back up. Why wasn't he fighting back or fleeing?

Looming over him, one knee wedged on the floor beside his ribs, she pressed her gun against his chest. "You've chosen the wrong homeowner to mess with, buddy."

He didn't respond. She couldn't make out his features, but she could see the whites of his eyes. He was conscious. He lay there, breathing heavily, arms out at his sides.

"I'm not here by mistake. You're the person I came to see."

Raven flinched. That smooth, commanding voice… The memory of it had stalked her in the wee hours of the night when she longed for sleep to overtake her.

She subconsciously dug the gun barrel deeper into the taut flesh beneath his collarbone. He grunted.

"Raven, it's me. Put the gun away."

Certain she'd fallen asleep in her bathtub and was having a strangely realistic dream, she slowly removed her flashlight from her utility belt. She shone the beam directly in his face and received a bone-jarring jolt.

She scrambled off him, holstered her weapon

and punched the hall switch. The overhead light illuminated the man lying prostrate on her floor. Her gaze started with the stained sneakers, sliding up the faded jeans encasing his long legs and the olive green canvas jacket over a black hoodie. A tiny scar was visible on his throat, earned from a careless swipe of a modeling scalpel. Her pulse rumbled through her ears like the river after a heavy summer rain. This couldn't be.

The serious, striking features belonged to Dr. Aiden Ferrer, esteemed architecture professor at Abbott-Craig University.

High, intelligent brow; unwavering, molten brown gaze topped with jutting eyebrows; straight, thin nose and lips that were often pressed together, indicating profound thought. A full beard hid the planes of his face and contrasted with the ashen cast of his skin. His black curls were disheveled and clearly hadn't seen a barber's scissors in quite some time. A fresh bruise was visible at his temple.

"You died. The car—the river—"

"I'm going to get up now, all right?" He took his time getting to his feet, his gaze fixed on hers. "Raven, listen to me. You're in danger."

She closed the distance between them, unable to resist touching his cheek. His eyes widened, and his breath hitched.

"I went to your memorial. I've been mourning you ever since that night…" Her knees went limp as noodles, and she put a hand flat against the wall to keep from falling.

He drew closer to assist her. She warded him off with a glare. He lowered his hand, his expression sad. "I regret putting you through that."

"Regret?" she repeated, incredulous. "What's going on, Aiden? Where have you been?"

"I witnessed the murder of a young man. A former student. The men responsible want me dead. Now that they know I'm alive, they'll come after you to get to me."

"What men?"

He opened his mouth to respond, then stilled, cocking his head to the side. "Did you hear that?"

Truth be told, she wouldn't have heard a black bear rumbling through her kitchen right now.

He brushed past her and, keeping to the shadows, went around to all of the windows checking for… She wasn't sure who or what exactly.

"How did you get in here?"

"Picked the lock." He surveyed the front yard, nervous energy radiating from him. That in itself was telling. Aiden had always been a steady, immovable presence. Not much ruffled him. "You should invest in an alarm system."

Raven intercepted him as he made to return to the French doors. "Aiden, stop. You need to tell me everything."

* * *

Raven took his breath away, and not by tackling him or aiming her service weapon at him. The woman he'd given his heart to was right in front of him, a living, breathing, vibrant, beautiful being. His memories hadn't done her justice. Long, rippling ebony hair framed her oval face and pleasant features. When on duty, she wove the strands into a tidy braid, highlighting her clear brow, straight nose and eyes the color of warm honey. Her lips were pink and inviting.

He could gaze at her for hours, days, years—he'd unconsciously lifted his hand toward her, and she jerked back, her eyes wary. She had a right to be wary of him now.

Frustration gripped him anew, along with the festering wound she'd inflicted. But no, now wasn't the time to revisit their past. He was here solely to warn her.

"In the weeks leading up to the crash, I discovered a cheating scheme involving students and the university registrar, Leonard Grunberg. He was accepting bribes—altering grades in exchange for cash. Because the registrar's office creates and maintains student records, Leonard has complete access. These students are members of our athletic teams—football, basketball, track, baseball—the list goes on."

"The general educational policy is that student athletes don't play if they can't maintain a certain grade point average," Raven interjected.

"That's right. As you know, our football and basketball teams generate millions for the university and the town. The students are pressured to perform well on and off the field. Their scholarships hang in the balance."

"The influx of fans for each game boosts the local economy," she said slowly. "They patronize hotels, restaurants, shops."

"Successful seasons help woo future athletes to our university," he added.

"How did you learn of this?"

"I had a student in my class who was really smart, but he didn't put much effort into his work. Tim ignored the opportunities I gave him to bring up his grade, and he failed the class. The following semester, I noticed he was enrolled in the subsequent class. It would be like trying to tackle Algebra Two after failing Algebra One. The professor wasn't sure how he'd gotten approved. I checked the grading system, and his grade wasn't the one I'd submitted. It had been changed to a passing one. I went to Desmond with my concerns, and he reassured me he'd look into it."

"Desmond Whitlock, the architecture department head? The one who recommended you for the position?"

He nodded, still reeling from the untenable truth exposed that very day. The man he'd respected and admired, the one he'd viewed as a mentor, had been a fake. A phony.

"I realized he hadn't done as promised when my path crossed with Tim's again. The professor told me that Desmond was still sorting things out. I assumed he'd gotten distracted with other duties. I decided to review my records and search for students who'd failed my classes. Of the ten students that year, eight of them continued through the program. I wondered how it could've happened and why. When I took the evidence to Desmond, he acted genuinely surprised and promised to investigate."

"But he didn't."

He shook his head. "I took it upon myself to approach one of my former students, Jay Crowell. Jay played on the football team his freshman and sophomore years. Between the practices and games, he couldn't keep up with the coursework. He dropped out of school altogether and wasn't sure if or when he'd return. Jay admitted that he'd gotten a tip from a teammate about Leonard. He said he paid Leonard on multiple occasions, and that he wasn't the only one, not by a long shot."

Her brows shot up. "Bribery is a serious offense."

"I doubt Jay realized that. He wasn't a student

any longer, and he probably figured that made him immune."

She tilted her head to the side, her gaze troubled. "Where's Jay now?"

"He's dead." Jay had been nervous that last time they'd spoken. His apartment had been broken into, and he'd suspected someone was following him. "We were meeting to discuss taking our information to the chancellor's office or even the university police. I heard a commotion in the backyard. I walked around the house and saw two men dragging his limp body toward the pool."

"Who?"

"I recognized Leonard Grunberg. Both wore masks, but Leonard's was askew. I saw the stag tattoo on his neck." He fisted his hands. "I wasn't sure if Jay was dead or not, so I confronted them. When I got closer, I realized I was too late." He got sick to his stomach every time he relived that night. "Leonard had learned of my snooping and, just the day before, offered me a slice of the pie. When I refused, he made threats against you. He'd done his research about me and my life, but he didn't know you'd ended our engagement."

Pain bloomed in her eyes. "I didn't tell anyone."

"I didn't, either." Aiden had hoped that, after some time to reflect, she'd change her mind.

He'd known Raven had lingering insecurities related to her dyslexia, and that his education and chosen profession were reminders of the trials she'd endured. He lived in the world of academia, a place of trauma and significant mental and emotional turmoil for her. She'd felt intimidated by his parents—both retired educators—and his stable childhood rooted in learning. She had been born and raised here in Serenity, a charming mountain town adjacent to the Great Smoky Mountains National Park, by a widowed mother who was too busy supporting herself and her daughter to worry about grades. Raven's mother had been dismissive of her difficulties, leaving her to deal with cruel classmates and teachers who assumed she was lazy.

Aiden hadn't realized the significance of her doubts. He'd been blindsided by her decision.

"I told him you weren't involved, but he didn't believe me. At Jay's house, Leonard lunged for me, threatening to strangle me like he had Jay. I escaped and reached my vehicle. He and his accomplice chased me through deserted streets." He pressed his hand against his midsection, as if he could will away the queasiness. "It was dark, cold and rainy. The roads were slick. As we approached the bridge, Leonard nudged my bumper, and I lost control. There was no avoiding the river. I remembered to roll down the window, and I unbuckled as soon as the car slid into the water. I shimmied out, and the current buoyed me downstream. The rain was coming down in sheets by then. That, combined with the lack of moonlight, prevented him from seeing me. Once I found something to hang on to, I watched as they stared at where my car went under. A passing vehicle stopped, and the driver summoned the authorities.

"I decided to lay low for a few days. Then the local news outlets reported that the authorities had searched the river and failed to locate my body. They assumed I was dead, and I saw an opportunity to buy more time."

She'd grown paler with each word out of his mouth. Her eyes, though, were a smoldering fire. "Thirteen months is a long time."

"Don't you see? It wasn't just my life on the line. Staying dead protected you." He reached for her out of habit. She stepped back, beyond reach.

"I'm an officer. You should've come to me."

The front door shuddered from a solid impact, and he pivoted on his heel, arms out to try to shield Raven from the unseen threat. Another blow followed the first. Raven pushed him between the ottoman and couch, crouched beside him and whipped out her weapon.

TWO

"Any guesses who's trying to destroy my door?"

"Desmond," Aiden said through gritted teeth. "I reached out to him a few days ago, thinking he'd be my ticket back to the land of the living. Realized I was wrong when he pulled a gun on me earlier today." He took a ragged breath. "Or it could be Leonard or his accomplice."

There wasn't time to question him further. The door wasn't going to hold much longer.

"We'll go out the back and escape along the river." Her body was sore after a full day in the saddle, but fresh stores of adrenaline provided vital awareness and a surge of energy. She crept to the French doors, turned to be sure he was following and received a shock. "Since when do you carry a gun?"

He crouched near the end table, a Smith & Wesson looking very comfortable in his grip. "I have a target on my back, Raven."

"Dare I ask if you have the necessary registration and permit?"

A muscle in his bearded jaw ticked. "It's best you don't."

Raven hardly recognized this harder, scruffier, grimmer version of the man she'd agreed to marry. The old Aiden had exuded an optimism that was refreshing to a cop who'd seen too much of the seedier side of humanity. He was wildly intelligent, passionate about his work and his students, thoughtful and kind. He hadn't owned a gun, much less known how to handle one.

Her ex-fiancé had come back from the dead a different person. Exactly what had he been up to this past year?

Raven unlocked one of the doors, pushed it open and grimaced as the bitter cold swept inside. She exited first, glad she hadn't gotten around to replacing the light bulb in the patio's motion-activated light fixture. Darkness cloaked them as they navigated the gradual, downward slope toward the river. Aiden had been to her house numerous times over the course of their relationship. He would remember the spacing of the live oak trees, the stone fire pit, turquoise deck chairs and small shed that housed her lawn mower and gardening tools.

At the river's edge, they turned east and hurried along the footpath. Lights from her neighbors' windows spilled into the yards. She hoped the Turons' German shepherd was put up for the night.

"I left my truck near the end of this road," Aiden told her.

"I didn't see it." There were only six houses along this stretch of the river, including hers. She would've noticed a random vehicle.

"I concealed it."

He said it casually, reminding her that living in the shadows was his norm. She removed her phone from her pocket.

"What are you doing?" He grasped her arm.

His touch seared through her uniform blouse. Longing slammed into her, and it was almost dizzying. Aiden was standing *right here*, a real man with a beating heart and breath in his lungs, able to return her hug, to shelter her against his chest, to brush his lips over hers...

"Raven."

She blinked, astounded she'd lost focus, even for a second. "Calling this in to Dispatch. We need backup."

"You're sure that's the right move? I have no idea who else is working with Leonard and Desmond. What if the wrong people learn about my return?"

As Raven opened her mouth to respond, a bullet whipped through the night and struck Aiden in the chest. He fell back against a tree with a grunt, his expression one of shock, and slid to the ground.

Raven cried out, and Aiden lifted his hand toward her. Dull pain encased his chest. He couldn't seem to catch a breath. Felt like someone had taken a baseball bat to his sternum.

She tucked her hands beneath his armpits and dragged him deeper into the strip of woods. "Please, God, not again," she whispered.

"Raven."

"Don't try to speak." She glanced behind her to search her neighbor's yard and uttered soft commands into her phone.

Aiden started to unbutton his jacket. His fingers were unsteady, so it was slow going. "I'm okay."

"You will be," she vowed. "They're rolling an ambulance to this location. I just have to hold him off long enough."

"I'm wearing a bulletproof vest," he rasped, fumbling with the hoodie zipper.

She knocked his hands aside and felt for herself. "Bullet's lodged in the plate. It saved your life." Eyes wide, she rocked back on her heels. "When we get to a safe place, you and I are going to have a long talk." Raven helped him to his feet and recovered the gun he'd dropped. "Sure you're okay?" Worry tinged her words.

"I'm good." The streaks of pain were hopefully from bruises and not busted ribs. The store clerk had informed him those were a few of the potential consequences.

Together, they hurried past the remaining houses. The footpath ended, and the river veered away from the street. The trees were more spread out here, and Aiden directed her to his vehicle, an eighties model Toyota 4x4 truck. He'd left everything behind when he went underground, including his former vehicle. He'd scrubbed a lot of greasy dishes in order to purchase this replacement.

He'd parked it between two magnolia trees. They knocked off the branches he'd used to cover the hood and windshield and climbed inside.

"Where to? The stables?" Their mounted police unit operated out of the stables where their horses were housed.

"Mason's out of town with his family. Silver is with his fiancée, Lindsey, and Cruz is probably at his favorite hangout, The Black Bear Café."

He'd met Sergeant Mason Reed and Officer Silver Williams. Both were solid, respectable men. "I remember meeting Lindsey once or twice. She was in charge of Silver's vacation cabin rentals?"

"She still is, only now she'll be part owner."

"Who's Cruz?"

"Part of our unit. He's from Texas. Joined our team after you, ah, disappeared." She fastened her seat belt. He eased the truck onto the street and turned on the headlights. "Let's go to the station. It's beside the fire department. Do you remember the town layout?"

"Is that near the Mountain Vista Resort?"

"Yes." She looked at her side mirror, her thick braid sliding over her shoulder. Dainty silver earrings caught the light. "I'm glad my neighbors didn't come outside to investigate. Are you okay to drive?"

"I'm sore, that's all."

She fell silent as he navigated the deserted secondary roads toward the main highway that stretched from the city of Maryville to Serenity and on to the national park. Light from passing streetlamps strobed in the windshield, creating flickering patterns on her navy uniform pants with silver side stripe and polished tall boots. One hand was fisted on her knee, while the other gripped her service weapon.

"I never used to worry much about your job," he said, his palms biting into the wheel. "Now that I've been shot at, I have a better understanding of the risks you assume each time you put on the badge."

"It's my chosen career. You're a civilian. That's the difference." She looked over at him. "How did you get into my house?"

"I jimmied the lock on the back door. Like I said, you need an alarm."

"Or a dog," she said drily, her brow creased as if he were a frustrating puzzle.

"I apologize for frightening you." He turned the heat knob as high as it could go. The old unit coughed in response. "And for putting you in danger. That was the exact opposite of my intentions."

She arched a challenging brow. "*That's* what you're apologizing for?"

"I—"

"We've got company."

His rearview mirror confirmed a vehicle was approaching at a high rate of speed. Up ahead, a short bridge led to the four-lane highway junction. He was forced to slow down, even as the shooter was gaining on them. He couldn't blast through the stop sign and possibly cause an accident.

Raven was on the phone again, informing Dispatch of their movements. There were no vehicles in the southbound lanes, so he gunned it through the median gap, made a hard left turn and sped toward town. The pursuer's car was newer and faster, and in no time, his headlights were blinding them.

"Where's our backup?" Raven said tersely.

"Look." He inclined his head to an unmoving line of glowing red car lights clogging both lanes. He had no choice but to slow down.

She tucked the phone against her shoulder. "Bad accident, they tell me. Four vehicles involved."

The speedometer needle lagged as he eased his foot pressure, and they came to an almost complete stop. "What now?"

"There are too many civilians." She scanned both sides of the four-lane and pointed to a bike path and picnic benches on her right. "We go on foot."

Aiden parked the truck on the road's edge, unfastened his belt and grabbed his gun from the bench seat. Raven exited her side, staying low and pivoting toward the oncoming car, weapon outstretched.

"I've got you covered," she said. "Run to those trees."

He hurried around the hood to her open door. Abandoning her while he sought safety went against his instincts.

"Go, Aiden," she ordered, her breath a wispy cloud. "I'll be right behind you."

Brakes screeched, the shooter's pickup truck jerked to a stop and the driver's door flew open.

"Go!"

Aiden's tennis shoes dislodged loose gravel at the highway's border, then pounded against the firm earth. He heard an exchange of gunshots behind him and would've turned back if not for her voice close behind him, urging him to keep going. They dodged cement picnic tables and garbage cans. He ignored the growing ache in his chest.

They left the picnic area and ducked behind two Dumpsters. Raven peered around the edge and got off a single shot.

She scowled. "Missed."

Aiden scanned their surroundings, which included a building that resembled an ice-cream cone, with a giant swirl for a roof. The walk-up windows that made up the middle section were dark. Beyond it, a bumper boat ride and go-kart track were also closed, probably for the winter months.

There was a lot of open area between the Dumpsters and the ice-cream hut—nothing but cold air between them and the shooter. They couldn't stay put.

Aiden found himself offering a disjointed prayer for protection, particularly for Raven. She shouldn't have to pay the price for his problems.

Once they reached the hut, they hunkered down beside the chipped stucco base. The windows above them immediately exploded, raining glass on their heads.

THREE

Raven instinctively ducked to protect her face from the spewing glass. When it had settled, she checked on Aiden. He appeared unharmed, though his pallor was concerning, as were the beads of perspiration on his forehead in the chilled February air. They hadn't removed his body armor. Could he be suffering from blunt trauma? Even if a bullet didn't pierce the armor, the expended energy could cause serious damage to his internal organs.

"Can you make it to that building?" She indicated the arcade grouped with the bumper boats and go-karts.

He nodded.

She let Aiden take the lead, intent on staying between him and the shooter. They raced past the fenced-in bumper boats and pool and beneath the overhang connected to the arcade. A bullet pinged off the fence post near her elbow. This guy was an excellent shot. Where was backup? Should she have reached out to Silver and Cruz?

"Here."

Kicking in the side door of the arcade, she nudged Aiden inside, activated her flashlight and searched for something to bar the way. The token-operated game machines were too heavy to move.

"Follow me."

She jogged between Skee-Ball and air hockey machines and took the stairs leading to the second floor play area two at a time. Aiden kept up the pace, and they nestled in between a pair of shooting games just as the door flew open. Raven switched off her light and, inching closer to the black metal railing, readied her 9mm.

Thanks to the streetlight outside, she could see the shooter's outline in the doorway. A baseball hat was pulled low over his eyes, and a camouflage neck gaiter covered the bottom half of his face. The gun in his hand was quite large, possibly a Desert Eagle, a semiautomatic that shot .50 caliber rounds. Her shoulder blades tightened, and her stomach knotted. A bullet like that could do irreversible damage.

His head cocked to one side, and he spun to look behind him. Sirens pierced the night.

He melted into the darkness. Moments later, blue and red lights swirled through the open door.

"I think he's gone," she murmured. "Did you recognize him?"

"From this angle, I couldn't get a good impression of his height or build. Could've been any of the three men."

"You can identify Leonard as being at Jay's home the night he died. Could Desmond be the other one? Maybe we're only dealing with two suspects."

"The masked accomplice was white, like Leonard, and shorter than both men."

Noticing Aiden's weapon, she frowned. "Better put that away."

He tucked it in his rear waistband, where it would be covered by his coat.

An officer darkened the doorstep, weapon and flashlight in his outstretched hand. "Serenity Police. Put your hands where I can see them."

"Officer Weiland?" Raven identified herself and slowly got to her feet. "I'm not alone. I have a friend with me."

The officer also holstered his weapon as he spoke into his radio. He shone the light on them. "We heard you had a shooter in pursuit. Either of you need medical assistance?"

"Aiden needs to be evaluated."

He used the railing to boost himself up. "I can't go to the hospital and risk the news media getting tipped off." He cleared his throat and shifted uncomfortably. "Besides, I've got limited resources now."

She hadn't thought about the practicalities. He'd lost his position at the university and everything that went with it, including a steady, comfortable income and health insurance. "I'll contact a paramedic friend of mine. He can meet us at the stables. If he says you need further assessment, you'll have no other choice."

"Agreed."

Raven told Weiland to cancel the ambulance request and gave him a description of the shooter, which wasn't much to go on. They descended the stairs, and Officer James Bell met them outside.

"The suspect got into his vehicle," Bell said. "Because northbound traffic is at a standstill, he drove across the grass median and sped the opposite direction. He's driving a late model gray Ford pickup. I got a partial plate and called it into Dispatch. Most of our guys are working the traffic accident, so they'll loop in the sheriff's department."

Because Serenity had a modest police department, the sheriff's department regularly provided assistance in the way of extra man power and the use of their crime scene unit.

Bell's gaze locked onto Aiden. "You look familiar. Have we met?"

Beside her, Aiden stiffened. "I've visited this area several times."

"He's with me," Raven said, infusing her tone with finality. "We'll be at the stables if anyone needs us."

"You aren't going to meet CSU at your house?" Bell's suspicions were aroused now. Hands on his hips, he was looking between them with raised brows.

"Aiden and I need a secure place to regroup for the time being."

"Aiden? Wasn't that your fiancé's name?"

Weiland had gone to the corner of the building, his phone pressed to his ear, probably updating the patrol unit's lieutenant. Raven leaned in and touched Bell's arm. He was a good man and an even better officer. "James, I need some time. I'll explain everything once I get a handle on the situation."

He rubbed his jaw, contemplating. "I'll stay here and protect the scene."

"Thank you."

Back at Aiden's truck, she asked for the keys. He hesitated only a moment before tossing them to her.

"Was Leonard driving a pickup that night?" she asked.

"It was a green Bronco."

"We'll have to find out if he owns more than one vehicle or if he bought something different."

Like their suspect had, she used the median to turn around. She drove about a mile and crossed the oncoming lanes to access a side road and alternate route to the stables. Raven studied every vehicle they encountered. If this was the full-on tourist season, which was roughly from April to October, the streets would be jammed. Thankfully, it didn't take them long to reach the mounted police stables, tucked in the middle of town, not far from hotels, shops and the police and fire departments.

The ivory metal building with green roof contained the horse stalls and tack and feed areas, along with their offices, locker rooms, meeting and break rooms. Beyond that, a sizable, tree-bordered paddock provided the horses with a place to exercise and graze. They spent the nights out there, too, if the weather was decent.

She stopped at the gate and punched in the code.

"You've updated security," he noted.

"We had to. Mason's now wife, Tessa, had Mafia thugs sniffing around last spring."

"Things don't stay the same, do they? Mason's married, and Silver's engaged." There was a distinct note of wistfulness in his voice, an unspoken wish that their lives hadn't taken this major detour.

Parking the truck between their horse trailers, she studied his profile in the orange-ish light that emitted from the building fixtures. Aiden wasn't the type of person who'd tolerate dishonesty in his professional or personal life. He was a man of integrity. That was why, after scraping the mounted police unit truck with his car during a Veteran's Day parade, he'd waited an hour for them to return. He'd wanted to give the driver his insurance information. He'd been determined to do the right thing.

Aiden had also been determined to get to know her. He had invited her for coffee, which she'd declined because she was on duty and also because she didn't date random strangers. But she couldn't help but be impressed by his integrity. More than a little bit interested, she'd looked him up online when she and her fellow officers returned to the stables. Learning he was a college professor had immediately dampened her interest. Too many bad memories were attached to the school setting and teachers, specifically. But when he'd sent the horses a basket of apples and carrots, she'd wavered. Mason and Silver had encouraged her to give Aiden a chance, and she'd listened.

Raven hadn't been searching for love, but it

had found her. She couldn't have known heart-break was in her future, as well.

"What happened with the thugs?" he asked, angling his body toward her.

"It's a long story, and right now, I'm more interested in yours."

Aiden's lips pressed together in a familiar fashion. She gathered it wouldn't be a pleasant account. How fun could it be to live as a dead man, pretending to be someone he wasn't?

He got distracted by the horses in the paddock, particularly the stocky black one with white bands around his ankles. "You're still partners with Thorn?"

She nodded, remembering those early days when he'd soaked in everything she taught him about mounted police and their horses. She'd gotten him used to the grooming and maintenance side of things before getting him in the saddle. They'd spent hours together in this building and on local trails. In fact, they shared their first kiss right beside the paddock gate.

"You can greet Thorn and the others later," she said gruffly, scanning the road and fields. Who knew where their fleeing suspect was? Perhaps he'd found a way to double back. "My paramedic friend promised to be here within the hour."

She unlocked the main entrance, deactivated the alarm and began turning on lights. The air was significantly warmer and tinged with the scents of hay and wood shavings. Inside the break room, located opposite the meeting room, she retrieved two bottles of water from the fridge and set them on the table.

"Let's have a look at the damage."

He heaved a sigh. After removing his canvas coat, he unzipped his hoodie. His slow, careful movements communicated his discomfort. When he started to release the body armor's side straps and let out a quiet groan, she brushed his hands aside and took over. Once the shoulder straps were unfastened, she eased it over his head.

"Better?"

"Much." He tugged his T-shirt collar down, revealing the beginnings of a massive bruise. But his skin wasn't broken. There weren't any unusual sounds associated with his breathing. He was alert, his pupils normal.

She pulled out two chairs, sat down and took a water for herself. He did the same, but he didn't open it. Instead he balanced the bottle on his knee. There were nicks and scrapes on his knuckles, some healed and some fresh.

"What do you want to know first?"

"Where have you been all this time?"

"Louisiana. In an isolated town where people don't ask questions." His eyes were hard, his face haggard. He had changed. He'd obviously lost faith in his fellow man. Had he also lost faith in God's goodness?

"While the police were towing my car from the river, I made my way to Pete's."

Pete Latimer was Aiden's oldest and best friend. They'd lived across the street from each other until they graduated high school. "He knew? All this time?" Leaving her chair, she paced beside the vending machines. "I spoke with him at the memorial. He put on an award-worthy performance."

"Pete wouldn't expose me, especially knowing the danger posed to you."

The service had been excruciating. Her eyes smarted just thinking about it. Mason and Silver had gone with her. They'd been kind and attentive to her, the grieving fiancée. She'd wrestled with the guilt of secrecy while reeling with the finality of Aiden's tragic death.

She didn't hear him come up behind her and startled when his hand settled on her shoulder and lightly kneaded her tense flesh. His touch launched out-of-control sensations in her middle, like fireworks spinning through the night sky. Raven squeezed her eyes shut, desperate to hold him, to be close again.

That was something she could never do. Giving in to the joy of learning he was alive would lead to more heartache and misery. He'd allowed her to mourn him. Even if she could forgive him, she couldn't move past the hurt and betrayal. Their differences still existed. He'd always be the brilliant professor with scholarly friends. She'd always be the learning-challenged girl who couldn't measure up to others' expectations.

"I'm sorry for hurting you, Raven." His breath stirred the tendrils at the nape of her neck, and she shivered. His rusty voice wrapped her in regret. "You don't know how many times I almost left my self-imposed isolation to come to you."

She fisted her hands and prayed for a clear mind. Shifting out of his reach, she faced him and willed the soft feelings away. "What's done is done. We have to move forward if we're going to see justice served. How did you wind up in Louisiana?"

Resignation became stamped on his features. He rubbed his hands down his face, scraping through the beard, and returned to his seat.

"Pete loaned me some cash and one of his vehicles. I drove to his lakeside cabin in Georgia, where I laid low for a few days before hiking into town and purchasing a bus ticket to Baton Rouge. Once there, I hitched a ride from a friendly trucker and got out in a town too small to map. I found a low-rent, long-term lease motel and a job at one of the restaurants."

"Doing what?"

"Bussing tables, cleaning dishes, emptying the trash."

Raven had trouble picturing him roughing it in a nondescript town. He'd achieved the highest level of education in his field. He'd published research and won scholarly awards.

"It was as tedious as you think," he said stoically, as though reading her thoughts. He'd always been good at that. "The residents were guarded at first, but most of them turned out to be decent, hardworking people."

There was a commotion at the front door, and they both turned as a man's voice carried down the hall. "Raven?"

Aiden reached for his weapon, but she put out her hand.

"In here."

Officer Cruz Castillo stormed into the break room, steam practically oozing from his ears. He advanced toward her ex-fiancé. "Who are you, and why have you put Raven in danger?"

"Whoa, slow down." Raven placed her hand on the stranger's chest. "Bell contacted you, didn't he? He promised to give me time."

"He said you've got a headache on your hands, and that this guy is all wrapped up in it."

She looked at Aiden over her shoulder. "This

is the Texan I told you about. Forgot to mention he's spicy. Comes from caring too much."

The officer's scowl deepened. He gave off a military vibe with his black hair shaved close to his head and lengthening into short strands on top, his erect posture and direct, *don't mess with me* gaze.

"This is Aiden Ferrer."

His brows lowered a notch. "The guy you were supposed to marry?"

"Yes."

"The one who died in a car accident?"

She pinched the bridge of her nose. "As you can see, he's not dead."

Aiden moved so that he could look them both in the eye. "I apologize for the danger I've brought to your town."

"Why didn't you stay dead?" Cruz challenged.

Raven kicked the toe of his boot and glared at him. "What kind of question is that?"

"A fair one."

Aiden sensed the two shared a close, trusting partnership. Whether or not that went beyond their mounted police work, he couldn't say. Nor did he have the right to an opinion. Their engagement had ended over a year ago. Raven had learned to live without him, while he'd never stopped thinking about her.

"I couldn't stay in hiding while the men who

murdered Jay Crowell—and attempted to silence me—went on with their lives."

"Aiden was a professor at Abbott-Craig University," Raven explained. "He has information that will cost people their jobs and potentially their freedom. Students will be put on academic probation or expelled."

She relayed the specifics in stilted phrases. This was as difficult for her as it was for him. Maybe more so. She'd suffered a shock and, thanks to him, had a target on her back.

The heat in Cruz's stare faded, but the wariness remained. "How did these people discover you were alive?"

"About two weeks ago, I reached out to my mentor and friend, the architecture department head, Desmond Whitlock. I thought he could help me. Connect me to the chancellor or another trustworthy member of the university faculty. Someone with the authority to discreetly look into Leonard's work activity. After he got over his initial shock, he agreed to meet with me and hear my story."

"Where did you meet?"

"A diner on a highway exit north of Morganton. I got the feeling I'd made a mistake almost as soon as we sat down. Desmond's behavior was off. After I'd shared my story, he accompanied me outside, pulled a gun and ordered me into his vehicle. I knew that if I obeyed, my actual death would soon follow. I created a diversion and managed to reach my truck."

"You drove straight here?"

"I had to warn Raven."

He hadn't thought beyond reaching her before Desmond or the others did. He hadn't considered what would or should happen next. Was he supposed to walk away? Hope that her police training was enough to keep her safe?

One thing he did know—now that he'd left the shadows, he couldn't resume the counterfeit existence he'd been leading.

FOUR

Aiden studied the photograph on Raven's fridge and wondered if he'd ever be that happy and carefree again. From where he was standing, the odds were slim. His adrenaline stores were depleted, and he was registering every ache and twinge in his body. He needed sleep—deep, restorative sleep that hadn't been possible in that seedy Louisiana motel. Probably wouldn't happen until Desmond, Leonard and their cohort were behind bars. Even then, peace would prove elusive. He hadn't had a chance to deal with his broken heart. He'd kept those feelings at bay as best he could and focused on planning his return.

"I'm going to need a new door, aren't I?" Raven entered the kitchen, followed by another of her unit partners, Officer Silver Williams.

After the paramedic had evaluated Aiden and given him the all clear, she'd contacted Silver and relayed the news of his return. The officer and his fiancée, who also happened to be Raven's friend and roommate, had met them here.

Silver, nicknamed such because he'd gone gray prematurely, had greeted him without the suspicion Cruz had displayed. He'd listened to the facts and immediately offered to help. Probably because they had history. As Raven's fiancé, Aiden had spent a substantial amount of time at the stables. He'd even been included in the unit barbecues.

"The damage is extensive," he said, walking to the sink and pulling the curtain across the window. "I can reach out to a buddy of mine and have him install a new one first thing tomorrow."

Lindsey circumvented the table to stand beside Silver. She nudged her red-framed glasses up her nose, her expressive brown eyes landing on Aiden again and skittering away. She was clearly having trouble digesting the fact that Raven's fiancé wasn't really dead, after all.

He would have to ask Raven what she intended to tell her friends about them. They were unaware of the breakup and would wonder why a reunion wasn't forthcoming.

Silver rested his hand on the pale quartz countertop. "Candace agreed to let Lindsey stay with her until the wedding."

"Under the circumstances, that's probably for the best." Raven glanced at Aiden. "Their wedding is in less than two weeks, on Valentine's Day."

"I heard about your engagement," Aiden said. "Congratulations."

Lindsey leaned into Silver's side. "Raven's in my wedding party. A bridesmaid."

Silver curved his arm around her. She smiled up at him, and they locked gazes, probably forgetting anyone else was in the room.

Raven glanced at Aiden and frowned. Was she wishing he'd stayed hidden in Louisiana? Did she have any feelings left for him? Or had she started cutting him out of her heart the day she returned his ring? The finality of his supposed death would've snuffed out any hope of future reconciliation.

Silver dragged his gaze away. "Officer Bell is taking guard duty tonight. You should get some rest. We'll discuss our next steps in the morning."

The crime scene unit had been clearing out when they arrived. They'd taken cast molds of footprints by the porch. Raven had given them his vest with the bullet lodged inside, and they'd promised to update him and Raven on their findings. He was convinced the shooter was either Desmond or Leonard, but the authorities couldn't rely on his hunches.

After everyone left, an awkward, disjointed silence descended. Raven's posture was like that of a soldier prepping for battle, but her face told of her weariness. She'd mentioned they'd had a full day of training, and he remembered how those sessions wore her down. Her dyslexia complicated some aspects of her police work. She had to expend a lot of energy just to focus on a task and not allow her active thought patterns to overwhelm or distract her. Processing information correctly was imperative, especially when reporting license plate numbers or driver's license information, so she checked and rechecked her work to the point of exaggeration. Accomplishing multiple things at once was also a challenge. But she never complained. She approached her career as she did everything else in life—with grit, determination and resourcefulness.

He used to knead the tension from her neck and shoulders, but he didn't offer to do that now. She'd nearly leaped out of her skin when he'd offered a commiserating touch earlier at the stables.

His stomach growled, and she raised her brows in question.

"How long has it been since you ate?"

"I skipped lunch and managed to down a few fries at the diner before I drove here."

"I had a protein bar hours ago." She opened the fridge and perused the contents. "Lindsey likes to cook and is happy to share. There's left-over shredded chicken. I could use that to make barbecue sandwiches."

He gestured to her uniform. "Why don't you go change while I assemble them?"

She considered for only a moment before accepting his offer.

Alone in her kitchen, Aiden set about preparing their meal. The cabinet contents weren't arranged in the usual pattern. There was zero organization, in fact, except for her collection of monogrammed travel mugs lined up like soldiers beside the coffee maker. He smiled to himself. Some things didn't change.

By the time she returned, he had the sandwiches prepared. He stuffed his hands in his pockets to keep from reaching for her.

Her damp hair fell to the middle of her back. Scrubbed clean, her skin was smooth and radiant. She'd changed into comfortable pants and a soft pink sweatshirt. The tangy, pleasant scent of apples curled around him, taunting him. Raven was an alluring combination of self-sufficiency and vulnerability, and his willpower was at a low ebb. He would like nothing more than to pull her into his arms and pour a year's worth of emotion into a kiss that would knock out the town's electric grid.

Pointing to the chopped radishes, cucumbers

and carrots, she gave him a rueful smile. "We have chips, you know."

He swallowed hard. "Really? Would they be in the freezer or maybe the linen closet?"

"As a matter of fact, they're right where I put them." She opened a deep drawer beside the stove and scooped out a shiny foil bag. "You still like this flavor?"

"I'm not as picky as I used to be." He'd barely scraped by on his income. The motel fees had gobbled up most of his meager wages.

Her features dimmed. He shrugged. "The restaurant cook taught me how to flavor beans ten different ways and pair them with rice, pasta or potatoes. Sometimes he'd take me fishing with him and his kids. After baking in the sun all day, we were rewarded with a fish fry. I didn't have money for indulgences, but I didn't go hungry."

She retrieved sodas from the fridge. "What did you miss most?"

"Steak and chocolate cake."

"You've obviously thought about it."

"I had a lot of time to think." The days had been long and draining, but he'd preferred them to the hours between his shift's end and bedtime—hours with no distractions besides the old television that broadcasted four local stations.

She scooted the chair opposite him from beneath the table and sat as if pushpins littered the seat.

"I didn't come back with expectations, Raven. I want to see Jay's killers punished, expose the university corruption and reclaim something of my former life, but your safety is my priority."

"We'll figure things out. Silver and Cruz are on board to help." Her eyes rounded. "Do your parents know?"

"No." His chest tightened. He'd hurt more people than just Raven. "I kept tabs on them through Pete. I called him once a month, each time using a different burner phone. You know they spend the winters in Tampa now?" At her nod, he continued. "I'd prefer to see them in person. As that's not an option right now, I'll have to call and explain."

She popped the tab on her soda, the clear sheen on her short nails glinting in the overhead light. "Pete checked in with me from time to time. Were you keeping tabs on me?"

"I didn't ask for details, and he didn't offer them. He only told me that you were strong, healthy and making it."

She set the can down with enough force to spill a few drops. "Did he tell you that I could hardly eat or sleep that first month? That I blamed myself for what happened? That I still have trouble sleeping through the night?"

His appetite went up in smoke. The raw grief ravaging her eyes speared him. He reached for her hand. "Blame yourself? Why?"

She snatched her hand away. She wasn't ready to talk. That much was clear.

"I'm sorry I hurt you."

"I understand that you did what you thought was right." The words were halting. She lifted her gaze. "Nothing has changed between us, Aiden."

Before the accident, he had planned to try to change her mind. He would've argued that their differences weren't a deal breaker. His circumstances had changed, however. He was homeless and jobless. He had nothing to offer her.

Raven held the water hose above the horses' trough and smiled at Thorn's antics. The Tennessee walking horse repeatedly bobbed his entire face in the water. "You're in a playful mood this morning," she said, her breath evaporating in curls of white smoke.

The other horses in the paddock grazed nearby as the sun peeked over the mountain ridges, shredding the white mist that hung suspended above the ground.

Thorn continued his play, and she let herself enjoy the moment. She couldn't have asked for a better partner. He was good-natured and dependable. They worked as a cohesive team on duty.

Off duty, he was a nonjudgmental companion, a natural anxiety reducer and calming presence. Something she desperately needed right now.

"You shouldn't be out here." Cruz strode up and held out his hand.

Raven reluctantly handed him the hose, but she didn't move toward the building. Aiden was inside. She'd rebuffed his offer to come outside with her. She'd needed a few minutes alone to gather her thoughts and tame her unbridled emotions. One minute she was elated to have him near her, the next dismayed.

She thrust her hands deep in her jacket pockets. "What would you say to a quick trip to Texas? Just you and me?"

His dark eyes studied her. "If I thought you were serious, I'd consider it. Wouldn't bother returning, though, since Mason and Silver would have my hide."

Raven looked out over the pasture, the mix of prickly evergreens and bare deciduous trees, the snow-dusted mountain ridges framed against a brittle pink sky. She wasn't sure what prompted the question. She didn't run from challenges anymore. She faced them head-on. With God's wisdom and strength, she was able to navigate life's roadblocks. Her learning disability, her father's unexpected death when she was twelve, her mother's inability to balance work with homelife, the demands of officer training and, most recently, Aiden's tragic "death." God had been her rock, confidant and helper her entire life.

This wasn't a surprise to You, Lord. You knew Aiden would waltz back into my life. I suppose it's part of Your greater plan. How am I supposed to feel? To react? To protect myself from further pain?

"You've suffered a shock." Cruz's voice invaded her thoughts. "A fiancé returning from the dead? Not many people can relate to what you're going through. But you have us."

She nodded tightly, embarrassed by the moisture blurring her vision. Crying alone in her bedroom? Completely acceptable. Crying in front of her partners, however, was something she tried to avoid.

Raven left the paddock and reentered the stables through the side entrance. She followed hushed voices to the meeting room, where Silver was taping photos to the whiteboard. Aiden was beside the far wall and the photograph mosaic of the state's mounted patrol units.

He'd removed his olive green jacket and stood with his arms crossed over his zipped black hoodie. He'd showered last night and borrowed a disposable razor. His beard was gone, revealing his strong jawline and firm chin. Loose curls tumbled onto his forehead, and he kept threading them out of his eyes. He would probably want to visit the barbershop soon. She would wait until he mentioned it, because she wasn't sure what he could afford. Maybe he'd been cutting it himself. She hadn't asked how tight his finances were, of course. He'd hinted of hardships but hadn't gone into detail.

Aiden noticed her in the doorway and straightened. Taller than her by several inches, he exuded a commanding presence that was impossible to ignore. She was certain he'd lost weight. Although he still stirred her appreciation, he looked like he could use a good dose of sunshine and infusion of vitamins and minerals.

Silver assessed her with concern, empathy darkening his eyes to a deep purple.

Movement registered outside the main glass door, and she spotted the patrol officers. "Why are Bell and Weiland here?"

"Since Mason's out of town until Friday, they offered to help."

Raven let them in and pointed them to the coffee. "There's a fresh pot."

Bell wasn't in uniform. He'd spent the night guarding her house and probably planned to make up for lost sleep after this meeting. He gave her a tired smile and made a beeline to the break room. Weiland was close on his heels.

Raven returned to the meeting room and chose a seat at the long table. Aiden lowered himself into the one beside her, and she caught herself staring at his hands. He had nice hands, wide and strong and tan. She realized the watch she'd given him for his birthday was gone. She'd wanted to give him something special, so she'd consulted with a few of his colleagues and been referred to an analog watch created for architects. A triangle, considered by designers as the most stable physical shape, dominated the face, and the band was Italian leather.

Lifting her gaze, she noticed his frown.

He'd vowed to wear it always. Had he lost it in the river? Or been forced to pawn it?

The patrol officers entered with their steaming mugs, and Cruz loped in a few minutes later, his nose and ears pink.

"Nice of you to join us, Cruz." Silver stared in exaggeration at his watch.

"I was hanging out in the break room," he quipped. "Got a new coloring book app on my phone. You should try it sometime."

Bell and Weiland chuckled.

"They're like teenage brothers," Raven explained to Aiden, "picking on each other and pretending they don't like each other."

"Who's pretending?" Cruz grunted with mock consternation.

Raven rolled her eyes. "It's worse when Mason isn't around. You'll get used to it."

Aiden had been quiet this morning. Had she been too blunt last night? While she'd battled guilt for keeping silent about their breakup, he'd no doubt been wrestling with his own. He'd kept his existence a secret not just from her, but his parents, friends and extended family.

Silver gave a brief rundown of Aiden's troubles at Abbott-Craig University, located in Morganton, twenty-five miles from Serenity.

"We wouldn't normally have a civilian sit in on a case meeting. Because you're an invaluable source of information and have an established relationship with Raven, I got Lieutenant Hatmaker's permission to include you as a consultant."

Aiden cast her a sideways glance. They hadn't yet discussed whether or not to disclose their relationship status. Did it truly matter right now? They had to focus their energy on capturing the perpetrators.

Silver tapped the board with a dry-erase marker. "Everyone, meet our suspects—Leonard Grunberg, Desmond Whitlock and a third unidentified male."

A forty-six-year-old Morganton native, Leonard was of average height but stocky. His severe crew cut didn't flatter his bullish features. Bushy brows protruded over ice blue eyes.

"Leonard is a medically retired marine," Silver said. "Joined when he was eighteen and served ten years before a bum shoulder ended his military career. No prior run-ins with law enforcement. He's worked for the university for more than a decade. According to his social media, he's a key member of a large survivalist group. He's an avid hunter and gun collector."

"He's been divorced for five years," Cruz added, consulting his laptop. "Photos of him looking cozy with a woman named Zara has popped up in his feed. The students' bribe money could be going to support his ex-wife and his new woman."

"Leonard is the only one I can positively identify as being at the scene of Jay Crowell's death." Aiden's jaw was tight, his brows tucked together. "I don't know the second man's identity, but it wasn't Desmond."

Silver cocked his head to the other photo. "Desmond, the architecture department head." The opposite of rough-around-the-edges Leonard, Desmond was a tall, thin, distinguished gentleman with rich brown skin, molten eyes and short black hair. "Again, no history of arrests. Model citizen. Involved in the community. Unlike Leonard, who's divorced, Desmond has been married for twenty plus years and has two adult children. His social media is sporadic and unremarkable. He likes to golf on occasion, join friends for drinks, that sort of thing. Aiden, what else can you tell us about him?"

Aiden released an aggravated breath. "Desmond's involvement came as a shock. In hindsight, I can see that his reluctance to act on my findings was a red flag. I missed the signs because I've never had a reason to question his integrity. He took me under his wing when I first hired on and became my sounding board. I wouldn't be the teacher I am today without him." He shook his head. "I don't know how long he's been working with Leonard or what would compel him to do so."

"He's willing to kill to protect his interests," Silver said. "He would've shot you if you hadn't escaped."

Aiden's head bowed and shoulders hunched. His mentor's betrayal evidently weighed heavily on him, and Raven crushed the urge to comfort him.

Cruz leaned back in his chair and snapped his pen cap on and off. "I'll look into the diner and find out if there are any security cameras in the vicinity. We need to get Desmond on camera."

"Are there any witnesses to corroborate your account?" Raven asked.

"It was deserted. Seems like the place is about

to go under. Desmond and I were the only pa-trons."

She frowned. They couldn't rely solely on Aiden's statement, especially since he'd gone underground, leaving his employer in the lurch and allowing his mortgage to go unpaid.

"Our shooter was using a Desert Eagle," she said. "Are you familiar with it?"

He nodded. "That's not what Desmond was carrying."

Cruz whistled. "Not your usual hardware. Good thing you were wearing that vest, Aiden, and the shot was taken at a fair distance."

Cold shimmered through Raven. That had been a close call, just as the car accident had been. God had His hand of protection on Aiden, and she couldn't begin to process the depth of her gratitude.

Weiland set his mug down and laced his fingers over his middle. "The encounter with Aiden could've rattled Desmond, and he called on his buddy Leonard to finish the job. They would've known he'd go straight to Raven."

She ran her finger along the plaid letters on her monogrammed thermos. "I don't have security cameras, but maybe one of my neighbors does. I'll contact them."

Aiden looked at Weiland. "Are there cameras at the arcade?"

"If there are, they likely aren't in use during the off-season," Bell inserted. "But I'll look into it."

"What happens this afternoon during the governor's visit?" Cruz asked Silver. "We can't withdraw from security duty."

Silver shrugged. "Aiden goes with us."

"He could stay in the truck," Cruz suggested.

Raven would be managing the spectators who turned out for the governor's speech. She wouldn't have eyes on Aiden.

"Leave him in the parking lot while we're elsewhere?" She shook her head. "The speech will take place on the courthouse steps. We can sneak him inside one of the offices. A courthouse security guard can stay with him."

Silver crossed his arms. "Do you have any objections, Aiden?"

"No objections." His gaze touched on everyone in the room, leaving her for last. "My presence has thrown a wrench in your schedule, not to mention put your well-being at risk. You have my deepest gratitude."

"We're happy to assist," Bell said. "Anything for Raven's fiancé."

FIVE

Raven hustled Aiden into her office, shut the door and sagged against it. "We have to decide what we're going to tell everyone." She waved her hand between them. "About us."

"It's your call. I guarantee Silver and Cruz have picked up on the subtle tension between us."

He certainly felt it humming along his skin, like an itch that couldn't be scratched, whenever she was near. Her mouth scrunched, bringing his attention to her lips, which were tinged with a sheer gloss.

She ran her hand along her hair, which was woven into her usual French braid. At this point in the day, it was pristine. Her navy blue, long-sleeved shirt with the Serenity Mounted Police emblem and black pants smelled like the dry cleaner's, but her apple-scented shampoo was detectable.

"That's natural, considering what's happened.

Essentially, it's no one else's business, but given Bell's assumption..."

"We could pretend you never returned my ring," he said, only partly in jest. "Until this case is resolved."

Sending him a look that substituted for a vocal rebuke, she pushed off the door, brushed past him and assumed her seat. The walls and shelves were white. The desk and chairs were white, too. Against this stark backdrop, plant pots, picture frames and a rug provided punches of orange, yellow and green.

"If it comes up again, I'll tell them the truth."

He sank onto the hard plastic seat across the desk from her. "Can I ask a favor?"

"What is it?"

"Would you mind calling my parents?"

Her forehead rippled in confusion. "Me?"

"It would be less shocking if you explain things as opposed to seeing my face straight out."

"I suppose you're right, although I haven't spoken to them in almost a year. They stumbled across some of my belongings when they were packing up your house." She pressed her lips together and busied herself straightening a stack of papers.

Had something happened between Raven and his parents? Something she didn't want him to know?

She consulted her watch. "Silver and Cruz are updating Mason on the case, and we have a while before the governor's visit. Are you ready now?"

His heart rate picked up. He ran his sweaty palms over his jeans. "Ready as I'll ever be."

Nodding, she opened her laptop and began typing. Her honey eyes flashed to him. "I assume you want to video chat?"

Aiden suddenly couldn't speak. He hadn't seen their faces in far too long. Rubbing his palms harder over his thighs, he nodded.

Her mouth lost its grimness, and her eyes became pools of understanding. "You're going to upend their world, but in the best way possible. Their only child is alive, after all."

The sound that came out of his mouth was somewhere between a squeak and a grunt.

She started the call. "As soon as I've broken the news, I'll give the three of you some privacy."

His mom answered, her greeting conveying surprise and curiosity. What it lacked was warmth and caring, which was unusual, given their connection. Raven reciprocated the tone. She was wary, on guard even.

He was so focused on contemplating the issue—and whether or not it had arisen before or after his disappearance—that he didn't follow the whole exchange. Before he knew it, Raven was standing and extending her arm, silently beckoning him.

Aiden's ears hummed as he took her place behind the desk. He registered his mom's tear-streaked face at the same time he heard the door click shut behind Raven. His dad shoved into the space, fingers touching the screen.

"I'm sorry," Aiden choked out. "I got myself into a jam, and I did what I thought was right in the moment."

His mom appeared stricken, and her hands were pressed to her mouth.

"Tell us everything," his dad ordered, his stern voice wobbling.

They both looked years older and stamped with weariness. The next three-quarters of an hour was grueling, and he was sure he experienced every emotion under the sun. He answered their questions and asked plenty of his own. They wanted to see him right away, of course, but he couldn't agree to a trip. And it wasn't safe for them to return. Leonard and Desmond wouldn't hesitate to use them as leverage.

There was a knock at the door, and Raven poked her head in. "Sorry to interrupt. We're going to leave soon."

"Five minutes."

She nodded and retreated.

"You're not going to pick up where you left off with her, are you?"

The acrimonious note in his mom's voice reinforced his earlier misgivings. "Did something happen between you that I don't know about?"

Her mouth became pinched. "You have a chance at a fresh start, sweetheart. I simply don't want you to make rash decisions."

His dad squeezed her shoulder. "Aiden has a lot on his mind. Be careful, son. Keep in touch."

Aiden ended the call with some nagging questions. He exited the office in need of a major caffeine jolt. Raven must've read his mind, because she met him with a granola bar and disposable coffee mug.

"You all right?" she asked, brow creased.

"I'm glad that's over." He sipped the strong, fresh brew. "Going forward, the rift I created can begin to mend."

She gripped her own monogrammed mug in one hand. "You and your parents are like three peas in a pod. Things will be back to normal in no time."

The phrasing sounded odd to his ears. Had Raven felt excluded? Had she not felt welcome in their family? Granted, the three of them were educators, and her history in the classroom was complicated.

Silver and Cruz emerged from the meeting room, preventing him from pursuing the subject.

"Just got off the phone with Mason. He offered to cut short his vacation," Silver said, folding his arms over his chest. "We convinced him not to. I also reached out to a friend of mine in the Morganton PD, Blake Jenkins. A detective. He wants to talk to you, Aiden. Get a formal statement about what you saw the night of Jay's death."

"I wrote down every detail I could remember as soon as I got to Pete's cabin. I didn't want to forget anything. Is it possible he'll reopen the case?"

"It was ruled an accidental drowning. According to Blake, there was plentiful evidence to indicate he was intoxicated."

"Jay didn't drink. He mentioned he was taking prescribed medication that didn't mix with alcohol." Anger burned in his gut. "Leonard and his buddy must've gone back and staged the scene after running me off the road."

"You said he lived in a rental?" Cruz asked. "What are the chances it's been sitting empty all this time? Any evidence would be diluted by new renters."

"We need to place Leonard at the scene or prove a connection between him and Jay." Raven's gaze settled on him. "No matter what we discover, Jay's death is not your fault."

Aiden wasn't sure he could see the young man's death any other way. His quest for answers had had a domino effect that impacted both strangers and the people he loved. He prayed no one else would get hurt because of it.

"This is where you'll wait out the event." Raven stood in the doorway as Aiden drifted through the office. His fingers skimmed the fireplace mantel while he leaned in to examine the woodwork, tilting his head back to take in the ceiling.

"What year was the courthouse built?" he asked, crouching to inspect a stained section of sheetrock.

"In 1905."

He was like this in every building of significant age. Raven had learned to give him space to satisfy his curiosity. She'd gleaned a substantial amount of knowledge from him and had even caught herself evaluating architectural features of buildings she entered.

He reached the almost floor-to-ceiling window and took in the view. This office, situated in the front right section of the courthouse, overlooked the sweeping porch and columns, wide steps and lawn, where spectators were already gathering. A portable, transparent podium stood in the middle of the porch awaiting the governor's arrival.

Aiden hadn't yet recovered from the conversation with his parents. He'd been quiet and distracted ever since. She hadn't probed.

Francis and Helen Ferrer were decent people, but although they'd been pleasant to her, they hadn't tried very hard to forge a friendship. Raven had sensed Helen's disapproval. Helen, a retired English professor, had clearly envisioned a different type of woman for her only son. Shortly before Aiden's accident, they'd attended Francis's retirement party. Helen's complaints to her friends had proven the catalyst for Raven's hasty decision to end things. Humiliated and hurt, she had let her own doubts consume her. She'd returned her engagement ring that night. Within a week, he was gone.

"A courthouse guard will be here soon. You should stay away from the window."

Shifting toward the antique desk, he brushed his hair out of his eyes and met her gaze. "You'll be a prime target out there on your horse."

Their greater visibility was usually a benefit. Citizens were much more likely to approach an officer on a horse than in a cruiser. The unit used that to their advantage, building relationships with community members and inviting confidence and trust.

"We're already a man down. I can't abandon Silver and Cruz."

He frowned. "You're wearing a bulletproof vest?"

"I am." She held her helmet by the chinstraps. "I've also got this sweet fashion accessory. I dubbed her Bessy."

The introspective set of his features altered as his lips quirked in a crooked smile. The combination of his twinkling eyes, tousled black hair and inviting mouth had her feet carrying her closer.

"Did the guys nickname theirs, too?"

"I tease Cruz that his should be called Chili Pepper. He thinks I'm ridiculous sometimes and isn't afraid to say so."

"He seems like a solid guy."

"Cruz doesn't let people close right away. He has to do his due diligence first and determine if you're worth his time and effort. If you're patient, you'll be rewarded with his friendship."

"I'm glad you have him and the others in your life, Raven. Knowing you had a strong support network kept me going on the toughest days."

"My law enforcement family and friends have been invaluable, that's true. But my faith even more so. God has been my ultimate strength and peace giver."

"I admire your steadfast trust in Him. I have to admit, I've experienced more than a few low points this past year." He leaned against the desk and folded his arms across his chest. "I acknowledge that my situation is of my own making. Even so, I questioned God. I wondered where He was and if He still cared."

Raven placed her hand on his arm. Beneath her fingers, she felt his biceps twitch. "He'll never stop caring about you, Aiden, and wanting good things for you. His Word promises that He'll never leave or forsake us."

His eyes softened, inviting her in. He covered her hand with his own, his fingers curling over hers, holding her captive. In this moment, she didn't want to break the connection. Her heart demanded impossible things… Spending lazy evenings on his porch, listening to records and watching the neighbors stroll past, camping in the mountains with friends, running together in the park, riding horses, frequenting food trucks.

Behind her, a throat cleared. She snatched her hand back and put distance between them. The guard entered the office, greeted her and introduced himself to Aiden.

"Thanks for helping out, Mitch." Raven slipped into professional mode. To Aiden, she said, "Mayor Chesney will say a few words of introduction before the governor takes the stand. His speech will last no longer than thirty minutes and will be followed by an informal meet and greet. We should wrap up here in an hour or so. He has other engagements in neighboring towns today."

Aiden slid his hands in his jacket pockets, resignation heavy on his shoulders. "After the horses are squared away, will we speak to your neighbors?"

"I have their numbers stored in my phone. I'll call them later today and ask if they'll check their video footage. See you in a bit."

Raven exited through the courthouse's side door and strapped on her helmet. Frail sunshine in the soft blue sky helped ease the chill a little. Her knee-high boots clicked against the sidewalk as she strode along the building to the lone oak tree, where she'd tethered Thorn. Silver waited for her astride his cremello horse, Lightning.

Cruz was on the far side of the lawn, closer to the library, handing out Renegade's bio cards to the kids. Each of the horses had their own, complete with their photograph and background info.

"Governor here yet?" she asked, releasing the lead rope and climbing into the saddle.

"The caravan arrived five minutes ago. Did you get Aiden sorted?"

"He's with Mitch." Nudging Thorn farther from the tree, she scanned the people streaming their direction from Serenity's central square. She recognized most of them—former classmates who hadn't left the area and their older parents, an assortment of teachers, shop owners, fire fighters, resort employees, campground attendants and more. There were a few new faces, most likely tourists getting in a visit before the true season started. She was on alert for anyone resembling Leonard or Desmond. Bell and Weiland had briefed the other patrol officers to be on the lookout. "Silver, I know this couldn't come at a worse time. Between managing the unit in Mason's absence and prepping for the wedding, you don't need to worry about my personal troubles."

"Mason will be home in a few days. As far as my wedding is concerned, nothing will stop me from marrying Lindsey." He flashed a brilliant smile that made his violet eyes dance.

Raven couldn't be happier for her friends. Silver had hired Lindsey to manage the vacation rental enterprise he'd started as a side business, Hearthside Rentals. The pair had worked together like a well-oiled machine. Raven, Mason and Cruz had known Silver and Lindsey were perfect for each other long before romance had occurred to either of them.

His smile faded, and his gray brows met over his nose. "Whatever you need, Raven, promise you'll reach out. We're here for you."

She bit the inside of her cheek to keep moisture from gathering in her eyes. Their support meant everything. "Mason said the same," she said, gripping the saddle horn. "He called this morning and again offered to cut his vacation short."

"Tessa wouldn't complain. Lily, on the other hand, wouldn't be very understanding. She's loving the beach."

Mason and Tessa's young daughter was adored—and spoiled—by all the unit members. Mason was the only one in their group with a child. Sorrow passed through Raven. She and Aiden had talked at length about how many children they wanted and how close in age they should be. They'd even picked out names. She could picture Aiden cradling a newborn, his face lit with wonder. Or helping a toddler walk across the living room, laughing with delight...

Her thoughts were determined to disobey the rules she'd set for herself. "I told him we have things handled here."

A six-piece musical ensemble started playing a celebratory tune. Mayor Chesney wove through the crowd at a leisurely pace, shaking hands and exchanging words with residents. The three rows of folding chairs angled toward the steps filled quickly, with the rest of the onlookers mingling on the faded grass.

Cruz put the bio cards away and guided Renegade away from the crowd. Behind them, the two-lane road leading to the middle and high school had been blocked off. A paved parking

area served the courthouse and library and also
the patrons of The Black Bear Café, which stood
alone in a large field near Glory Pond. Sections
of the pond were visible between the trees and
vacant picnic tables. The bike and boat rental
shop was locked up for the season. No one loi-
tered there or near the public restrooms.

Raven's gaze kept straying back to the office
where Aiden was waiting. She didn't like that he
was out of her sight. There were too many scenarios in which this could go wrong. She called
up a mental layout of the courthouse again. Had
they thought of every contingency?

Thorn bobbed his head, a gentle reminder to
stay grounded in the present. *Pay attention to
your actual surroundings, not imaginary ones.*
He read her nonverbal cues, and she had to be
sure to give the right ones.

The governor and his entourage approached
from between the library and courthouse. Mayor
Chesney broke free of the crowd and strode forward to greet them. The politicians shook hands,
and Chesney ushered the governor toward the
porch.

The music faded, and the mayor addressed the
crowd. Raven tuned out his words as she did a
sweeping scan of the area. There were people
in the square's parklike center, patrons of the
shops and eateries who weren't inclined to at-

tend the event. A police cruiser was blocking vehicle traffic at the juncture of the nearest row of shops and the center section. A uniformed officer stood nearby.

Applause sounded as the governor assumed the podium. Several times during the speech, Raven's gaze shifted to the window behind his right shoulder, as if she could probe the interior with her eyes. But the historic building's second story porch cast deep shadows. As he was making his closing comments, she caught sight of Aiden at the edge of the frame. She stiffened. He wasn't supposed to stand so close to the window.

Silver's mount shifted closer. "Blue van."

She twisted in the saddle. A rusted blue utility van was ambling behind the shops closest to the pond. The driver had skirted the blockade and was approaching their position at a slow crawl. Lieutenant Hatmaker left his cruiser and stretched out his arm, palm up. The driver applied the brakes. But when Hatmaker got close, he gunned it, swerving toward the trees and the boarded-up rental shop.

Silver radioed for Cruz to stay put while he and Raven assisted Hatmaker. The horses broke into a canter and quickly overtook the lieutenant. The van completed a U-turn, bumbling through the grass and almost plowing into a fixed garbage can. A cruiser with its lights flashing pulled out from behind Spike's Café. The van driver again swerved, tires peeling as he attempted to escape.

Was the guy impaired? Had he meant to disrupt the governor's speech? Or was he their third suspect?

As Thorn thundered beneath her, his muscled legs eating up the ground, she had a nagging feeling she shouldn't be leaving Aiden.

She radioed Cruz and asked for an update. "Governor is finished," he said. "Crowd's dispersing."

"Stay with Aiden?"

"Affirmative."

Two sheriff's deputies turned off the highway and blocked the van. They emerged from their vehicles with weapons drawn. Silver went right and she went left, so they fanned wide on either side.

Her hand went to the Glock at her waist as she tugged on the reins. Through the driver's window, she could see the man's profile. Definitely not Leonard or Desmond, but that didn't exclude the possibility of a link between him and Aiden.

The deputies repeatedly ordered him to show his hands. He finally complied, and one of them cautiously approached the driver's side door, yanking it open and tugging him out.

She nudged Thorn closer so she could hear the conversation. Then her radio crackled.

"The guard brought Aiden outside," Cruz said tersely. "I don't like—" He broke up, and shots rang out. "Shots fired at the police!"

SIX

The gunshot blast incited chaos. People scrambled for safety. Most fled toward the square, the opposite direction from where the shots originated. The governor's security detail herded him and Mayor Chesney inside the courthouse.

Cruz wove through the chaos toward Aiden and the guard, Mitch.

"Watch out," he warned those crossing Renegade's path. "Out of the way."

Mitch groaned, and Aiden realized he was no longer standing beside him. The bald-headed man was sprawled on the steps. Blood seeped from a wound in his side.

Aiden discarded his jacket and, removing his hoodie, pressed the wadded material against the wound. While he wasn't squeamish, seeing a gunshot wound firsthand was very different from seeing one on a screen. "Hang on, Mitch."

Renegade's hulking body was suddenly there,

the horse acting as a barrier between them and the crowd.

"We need an ambulance!" Aiden called up to Cruz.

"They're en route." His hard gaze scoured their surroundings. He had his service weapon drawn and ready. "Keep pressure on that wound."

Aiden needed no prompting. The bullet meant for him had struck an innocent man instead. Flashbacks of that night at Jay's filled his mouth with dread. Would a second person's death be on his shoulders?

A rhythmic pounding vibrated the earth, and Raven and Thorn streaked across the lawn in pursuit of the shooter. They moved as one entity, fluid and connected and focused on their task. Silver and his mount weren't far behind.

Watching Raven ride straight into danger made his throat constrict. He'd admired her choice to serve and protect her community. He'd seen her in action at parades, school functions and even traffic accidents. But this... He'd been shielded from the very real hazards of her career. She helped defend the innocent from evil. She chased down men and women who didn't value human life and who wouldn't blink at harming a law enforcement officer.

Aiden's prayer life had fizzled as frustration with his circumstances mounted. Now, quick pleas rose to his lips. *Lord Jesus, please save Mitch's life. Please protect Raven, Silver and the other officers.*

He shifted on the cold, hard steps and noticed Mitch had closed his eyes. "Mitch? You still with me?"

He licked his lips in between labored breaths. "Yeah."

Red began to pool beneath the prone man. "Cruz, where's that ambulance?"

Cruz looked down from his perch, and his forehead bunched with concern. He used the radio on his shoulder to contact Dispatch. The piercing shriek of sirens was a welcome sound.

When the paramedics arrived, Aiden gladly gave Mitch into their capable hands. He backed away, belatedly noticing the blood on his hands.

His thoughts drifted to Jay again. The young man had died alone, with no one around to help or comfort him. *Please don't let this end in another death, Father.*

"Aiden."

He whipped his head up and found Cruz studying him.

"Stay close." He indicated a spot near Renegade's side. "From what I'm hearing on the comms, our shooter hasn't been apprehended."

Through the distant trees, he spotted Raven astride Thorn. They rode around the slate gray pond before heading back to the courthouse. The annoyance in her features changed to horror when she noticed the blood on his hands.

"It's not mine," he said in a rush. "Mitch got hit. He's on the way to the hospital."

"How bad is it?"

"He was awake and coherent," Aiden supplied.

"There's no sign of the shooter," she told Cruz. "It's like he vanished into thin air. SPD and the sheriff's department will establish a perimeter and start interviewing witnesses and searching buildings."

"Now that you're here, I'll join the search." Cruz nudged his mount into action, and he approached the nearest uniformed officer.

Raven dismounted and gestured to the unit truck and horse trailer parked across the road. "You and I are going to the stables, and we're going to stay there until we get the all clear."

"Will you get updates on Mitch's status?"

"Someone from the department will head over there. I'll find out who once we've got Thorn settled in his stall." She loaded Thorn, promising the animal that water and a snack were a short ride away. He flicked his ears and tail as if to thank her.

She was tense behind the wheel, checking the side mirrors and scanning the roads they passed. Aiden's tension coiled inside. When would the next attack happen? Would they be ready? Would more people get hurt?

"Why would anyone choose to launch an attack in a place that's crawling with law enforcement?" The fact that Leonard and Desmond had gotten away with their crimes proved they weren't inept.

She shrugged. "Arrogance? The thrill of trying to outwit police? I've read—listened to, actually—a book or two about criminal psychology. I also subscribe to several crime-related podcasts, but I'm no expert. Criminals do things for a lot of different reasons. Sometimes they make sense in a weird sort of way, and sometimes they don't."

Inside the stables, Aiden used the locker room sink to wash his hands and face. His hoodie had gone in a garbage bin outside the courthouse. His green jacket, which he'd tossed carelessly to the steps, now sported bloodstains. He couldn't afford to replace it, so he used the dispenser soap to try to clean it. His parents had regretfully informed him that they'd used the profit from his house sale to pay off their condo in Florida. The savings he'd managed to cobble together from his restaurant gig would carry him for maybe a month. He couldn't exactly ask to resume his teaching position at Abbott-Craig. He couldn't get any job while there were bullets with his name carved on them.

Leaving the jacket to dry, he left the locker room and rejoined Raven at the stalls. She was in the process of removing Thorn's tack. She'd taken off her helmet, and her braid trailed between her shoulder blades. Little wisps curled around her face and grazed her neck. He longed to move in close, wrap his arms around her and drop a kiss on the nape of her neck. How he'd yearned for her company all these months...he'd replayed their relationship from beginning to end countless times. Those memories had kept him grounded.

As if sensing his presence, she turned and met his gaze. Her lips parted. Her eyes deepened to the color of warm teak, inviting him closer. She may have buried him thirteen months ago, but she hadn't completely buried her feelings for him. He was sure of it.

Aiden slowly crossed the distance, heart rate picking up speed, palms damp and mouth dry. He didn't stop until he was close enough that she had to tilt her head back or else stare at his collarbone. He reverently trailed his fingers from her temple to her chin. Her lower lip trembled. He cupped her jaw, his fingers sliding into her hair.

Raven took hold of his wrist, fingertips pressing into the soft underside. "Don't."

The plea contrasted with her body language. Still, he respected her wishes. Regret battling unmet yearning, he lowered his hand to his side and took a step back.

She presented her back to him and resumed her work.

"What can I do to help?" he asked softly.

"Get him some water."

They worked in silence, the sounds magnified beneath the elevated ceiling. When Thorn was enjoying his supper, Raven dusted off her pants, took a long draw from her water bottle and adopted her no-nonsense demeanor.

"We have to be vigilant, Aiden. We can't allow sentiment or loneliness to cloud our judgment. There are people out there who want you dead, and me by default. My team is putting their lives on the line. Distractions could prove deadly. Do you get what I'm trying to say?"

"You're happy I'm not dead, but you're sticking with your original decision. You don't want a relationship with me."

She grimaced. "It would be very easy to succumb to old patterns. We never had trouble in the affection department. But you and I were never meant to work long term."

Aiden wasn't going to attempt to dissuade her. He was no match for lifelong, ingrained insecurities. And he wasn't going to apologize for who or what he was.

"I won't let it happen again."

"Mayor Chesney is furious. Today's debacle reflects poorly on our city and department. I should've been informed about the active threat." A vein in Lieutenant Hatmaker's temple bulged as his tirade continued. He'd blown in like a summer storm just as Silver and Cruz had finished grooming and feeding their mounts. Stationing himself in the middle of the wide aisle, he'd launched into a scathing lecture. He jabbed a finger at Silver. "When you requested to add Aiden Ferrer as a consultant on a case, you failed to go into particulars. Big mistake."

Raven squared her shoulders. "With all due respect, sir, this case landed in our laps late last night. We scrambled to contain the situation and protect Aiden while piecing together a picture of what we're dealing with. It was too late to withdraw our services for the governor's visit or request another unit to replace us."

"Thanks to you three," Hatmaker waved his hand over them, "video footage of the governor and mayor fleeing into the courthouse is circling the internet. We have a shooter on the loose and a guard in the hospital."

Aiden ceased pacing and opened his mouth

to protest. Raven shot him a quelling look. He snapped his jaw shut, but he didn't look happy about it. She wasn't happy, either. The lieutenant was difficult to work with under the best of circumstances. He didn't fully understand how their unit operated. She suspected he thought they were unnecessary.

The older man fixed his steely stare on her. "Officer Hart, the only reason you're not taking leave is because Sergeant Reed is out of town. I'll allow you to remain on duty, but you won't be taking part in any more public events."

"The calendar is clear of those until the end of the month," Silver supplied, chin out, hands locked behind his back. "We'll take every precaution during our regular patrols."

"If the public is put at risk again, I'm shutting this unit down until the case is closed." Pivoting on his heel, he marched out of the stables.

Aiden's cocoa brown eyes stirred with unease. "Can he do that?"

"I don't want to find out," Cruz muttered, rubbing his hand over his short hair. "I would like to know how the shooter got in and out of the area without being seen."

Raven shared the sentiment. Law enforcement had interviewed dozens of bystanders. They'd searched the buildings and surrounding properties, including the spot where the shots were believed to be fired from. Not a single bit of useful information had materialized.

"Maybe security feeds will give us something," Cruz said, unbuttoning his uniform blouse and revealing the bulletproof vest underneath. "Bell is at the courthouse reviewing them."

"Or the news footage," Silver said. "Reporters were there from our newspaper, as well as the local news channel. I'll reach out to them."

"Thanks, Silver. Aiden and I will be in the meeting room."

After getting Thorn settled, she showered and changed into jeans and a teal sweater. She'd blow-dried her hair and left it hanging loose. Aiden had done a double take when she'd emerged from the locker room. A tactile person, his fingers had often found their way to her hair, whether they were sitting in church, a movie theater or on one of their couches watching TV.

Her skin heated anew, remembering the close call. He would've kissed her if she hadn't stopped him. Stopping him had taken every ounce of willpower she had.

Raven retrieved her laptop from her office and brought it to the long table in the meeting room. Aiden was right behind her, and he took the chair beside her so he could see the screen. His lean frame so close to her was a temptation. The scent of his woodsy aftershave clung to his skin. He'd changed into a clean, short-sleeved shirt. The light blue color accentuated his black hair, dark eyes and golden skin.

"What happened to the watch I bought you for your birthday?" she blurted.

His eyes flared in surprise, and the tips of his ears reddened. "I, ah, was forced to pawn it."

"I see."

"I wouldn't have parted with it if it hadn't been absolutely necessary."

"No need to explain. I understand."

She returned her gaze to the screen and began to type, but her thoughts remained stubbornly on Aiden. His impulsive decision to go underground had exacted a tough penalty. He had very little left of his former life.

Silver entered the room. He'd exchanged his uniform for his customary head-to-toe black. One thing that had changed since falling in love with Lindsey? He'd stopped wearing long sleeves and gloves year-round. He no longer seemed to care what others thought about the scars on his arms and hands.

"I'm going to order delivery," he said, holding his phone up. "What are you in the mood for? Pizza? Burgers? Cashew chicken?"

She looked at Aiden. Italian food used to be his favorite. Was it still? "Your choice."

"Whatever you decide is fine. Just let me know how much I need to chip in."

"This is on me," Silver said.

Cruz breezed into the room. "In that case, let's order the most expensive thing on the menu," he quipped.

They ultimately decided on pizza. Easy to eat, minimal cleanup and delicious.

Silver slid out the end chair, lowered himself into it and typed out a series of texts. Cruz leaned over his shoulder for a better look.

"I don't believe it," he said, whistling. "Silver uses the kissy face emoji."

Silver continued typing. "You're just jealous because you haven't found a woman willing to put up with you."

His expression shuttered. "I'm not interested in getting bossed around and having to report my every move to someone else." His tone had a false lightness, and there was a hint of pain in his eyes. He sent her a pointed stare, a silent reminder to keep his past secret. Raven was the only one in town who knew about Cruz's failed marriage and the reasons he'd left Texas.

Silver put his phone facedown on the table. "It doesn't have to be that way. Ask Aiden."

There was an awkward silence as Cruz's gaze cut toward Aiden.

Silver's gaze assessed them. "I didn't mean to

bring up a sticky subject. You obviously haven't had time to work through matters."

Aiden's gaze bored into Raven's. "We can't avoid the issue indefinitely."

Brushing her hair behind her shoulder, she lifted her chin. "Aiden and I ended our engagement before the accident."

The men exchanged confused looks. "Why didn't you tell us?"

She hesitated, and Aiden jumped in. "I asked her to keep our breakup quiet. Truth is, I had every intention of mending things. I'd hoped for a reconciliation."

Her stomach balled into an uncomfortable mass. "This occurred just days before he was run off the road. I should've told you the truth."

"It's your business." Cruz stared at Aiden, as if warning him to tread lightly. He obviously didn't trust him.

"The important thing is eradicating the threat against you. Then you can return to your normal lives…whatever that might look like for each of you." Silver opened his laptop, a signal the personal topic was closed. "We're dealing with one shooter at the scene today. Is he the same man from last night? The incident with the blue van appears to be unrelated. Driver is a drunken tourist who unwisely thought he was good to operate a vehicle."

The tap of keyboard keys filled the room as they scrutinized their suspects' online activity.

"Desmond's not our guy," Cruz said. "He conveniently posted a live video from campus at the same time as the shooting."

Raven leaned forward in her seat. "Listen to this—Leonard frequents a popular gun range and is part of a shooting club. I wonder if some of his fellow club members would be willing to help him get in and out of the area unnoticed?"

Silver arched a brow. "That person would have to be okay with shooting into a crowd of civilians."

Cruz twirled a marker in his fingers. "There would've had to have been a getaway car, which no one has confessed to seeing."

"Considering Leonard's hobbies and skill set, he probably knows how to conceal himself well," Raven said. "The shots came from the strip of woods adjacent to the parking lot across from the courthouse and library. That section extends behind the Black Bear Café and continues for maybe a mile, where it joins more woods and farmland. He could've camouflaged himself and stayed in place while law enforcement searched around him."

Silver looked thoughtful. "He could've seen it as a challenge. Something to brag about to his survivalist buddies. We'll go back at first light."

Cruz linked his fingers behind his head, elbows flared out. "Are there any obvious connections between Leonard and Jay? Maybe Jay worked in the registrar's office as part of a work-study program?"

"I'm not seeing any. There's very little mention of the university in Leonard's social media," Silver replied. "If I were him, I'd be careful to keep any links between me and the participating students out of the public eye. We need to have some conversations with people in Jay's life, starting with his landlord and neighbors. Aiden, what sort of records did you keep? Can you get your hands on them? Proof that our suspects have something to hide, something worth murdering someone over, would go a long way toward getting Jay's case reopened."

"I compiled a list of the original eight students who failed my entry-level class but continued through the program. Student assignments are submitted online in a sort of vault, if you will, and stored for five years. I accessed the vault and took screenshots of their work, which showed their failing grades. They must've become aware of their oversight, because by the time I went in to retrieve the last student's work, it was too late. They'd changed the grades."

"Was this before or after Leonard offered to cut you into their scheme?"

"After. The night before Jay's murder."

"Your refusal made him nervous. There's a good possibility you were next on his hit list, but you interrupted his plans when you showed up at Jay's."

"I stored the info on two flash drives. One I hid at my home and the other in my office inside the Art and Architecture building."

"Your house was sold, along with most of your furniture and clothing," Raven said. The process had been overwhelmingly sad. "The university staff would've cleared out your belongings to make way for the new professor."

"My parents said they boxed up some of my personal items and stored them in their basement. My mom couldn't bear to part with those things. I stored the drive in my record player. She's not sure if it's there or not. Hopefully it is, because it's unlikely the one I hid in my office is still there."

"You're not returning to Morganton alone," Raven asserted.

"Maybe it would be for the best," he responded. "You'd be safer with your unit, here in Serenity."

"The last time you were there, they almost succeeded in killing you. These men have proven they'll go to any lengths to protect their money-making scheme, hold on to their jobs and stay out of jail. You need backup, and I'm the best person to provide it."

Returning to his parents' home wouldn't be a walk in the park. It was last place they were together as a happy couple, before everything fell apart. The university presented its own obvious challenges. Emotional discomfort was a small price to pay if it meant keeping a watchful eye on Aiden.

SEVEN

The following evening, Raven drove the unit truck to Morganton, stopping at the community center before she and Aiden went to his parents' house. She parked close to the side entrance. "You don't have to come inside." The engine hummed, the vents blew out hot air and Pat Benatar crooned about strangers in the night. "One of the volunteers can help me unload the boxes."

In answer, he opened the door, got out and headed to the back of the trailer. She removed the keys from the ignition, unlatched the door and swung it open.

After a day of her usual duties, which included six hours in the saddle patrolling Serenity's parks and shopping centers, she'd received a call from her church secretary asking her to pick up the nonperishable food items the congregation had donated for the Helping Hands Kitchen. They were preparing for the church-wide Valentine's

Day banquet, she'd explained, and the donations had to be moved out right away.

As Raven was the one who'd organized the donation drive, she couldn't exactly ignore the request. They'd already planned a trip to Morganton this evening to search Aiden's parents' home. The quick pit stop wasn't an inconvenience. It did, however, add another layer of emotional trauma. Volunteering together had become as integral to their relationship as camping, music and art appreciation and horses.

If Aiden was surprised she was still an active volunteer with the organization he'd introduced her to, he hadn't let on. Helping Hands served free meals each week to families facing food insecurity. Aiden had started helping out in high school and had gotten close with the organizers, twin sisters Greta and Gwyn Coates. He'd referred to them as his adopted aunts, and they certainly treated him like family. Not long after he and Raven started dating, he'd invited her along on his weekly rotation, and she'd never stopped coming. They'd done everything from cooking and serving to wiping tables and taking out garbage.

Before climbing inside the trailer, Raven took a cursory look around. She didn't anticipate trouble. Cruz was already sitting on Leonard's house, and Silver was surveilling Desmond. The officers were in position and would alert them if either suspect made a move. That way, she and Aiden could deliver the boxes and then search for the flash drive without having to look over their shoulders every five minutes. The sun had already set, and streetlamps provided light for the surrounding businesses and parking lot. Nothing set off her inner alarm.

She went in and began pushing the stacks closer to him.

"How are the aunts?" he asked.

"Just celebrated their seventy-fifth birthday and still going strong." She chuckled. "They have more energy than I do. When I asked them what their secret was, they said a slice of chocolate cake every day."

He laughed and hefted three cardboard boxes into his arms. "Typical response. Chocolate is king in the twins' minds. You have to admit, their triple chocolate cake is unmatched."

"I can't argue with that." Raven stepped out of the trailer with her arms full. At the door, she pressed the bell with her elbow. "Maybe I should go in first and warn them—"

The door swung open. A diminutive woman who could've stepped from the 1950s stood in the bright hallway. "Raven! What's all this?" Her eyes squinted. "Who's your handsome friend?"

Aiden set the boxes down and removed his cap. "It's me, Aunt Gwyn."

Her gasp echoed through the night, and she clasped her pearls. "Aiden Ferrer?"

"In the flesh." He gently wrapped her in his arms. "It's good to see you."

She fiercely returned the hug. Dabbing at her eyes with a handkerchief she produced from her apron pocket, she ushered them inside. "Wait until Greta sees you. She'll have a fit."

Greta was in the kitchen babying a stockpot of what smelled like beef stew. Her spoon clattered to the linoleum. She didn't wait for him to initiate a hug.

"Sit down and tell us everything." Gwyn was already removing a tray of chocolate cake from the fridge.

Aiden smiled over at Raven, his eyes soft, reminiscent. How many times had they ended a shift with cake the twins had reserved for volunteers? Greta and Gwyn had regaled them with tales of their childhood in the foothills of the Smokies.

She gestured to the hallway. "I'll get the rest of the boxes. Our church members really came through, ladies. We have enough to last the rest of the month and then some."

"The Lord always provides." Greta wagged her finger.

Aiden did a half turn toward her. "I'll help you."

"Stay. I'll grab someone from the dining hall." Raven spun on her heel, exited the kitchen and followed the sounds of conversation and laughter. The dining hall was a lively, cheerful space, a manifestation of the twins' good will. People sat at long tables draped with red-and-white-checkered cloths, already tucking in to their hot meals. She beelined to the serving table.

"Ladd?"

The young man with strawberry blond hair was stationed behind bins of mashed potatoes and gravy. He looked up and waved. "Hey, Raven. I didn't see your name on the schedule."

"I'm here dropping off donations. Can you lend a hand?"

"Sure." With a word to the other helper doling out food, he tossed his plastic gloves in the garbage. "Most everyone has been served, so they won't miss me."

"I have a surprise."

"It's not my birthday." Ladd's brows did a funny dance. "Is it for Valentine's?"

"Not that kind of surprise." At the door to the kitchen, she paused. "Go on in."

Raven watched Ladd's face do contortions as he recognized his former professor and mentor. "Dr. Ferrer? Is that really you?"

Aiden jumped up from his seat, the generous slice of cake forgotten. "Ladd." Fondness underscored the confusion in his voice. "What are you doing here?"

"That's my question."

Aiden gave Ladd a vague answer without going into details. "How's school? And how is it that you're volunteering here?"

"School's no joke. I spend most of my time making parti designs and 3D models. But I make a point to come here at least once a month." Ladd's voice dipped. "Some of the other students and I approached Officer Hart at your funeral and asked what we could do to honor your memory. She told us about Helping Hands."

Gwyn piped up. "They're hard workers, too."

"They come for the cake," Greta said, a mischievous smile adding more creases to her face.

Aiden cleared his throat, and he surreptitiously wiped at his eyes.

"I'm glad you're back, Dr. Ferrer." Ladd gave him a lightning-quick hug, red spreading across his cheeks. "I can't wait to tell everyone."

"As soon as it's feasible, I'd like to meet with the student volunteers," Aiden said. "We'll get on the schedule for the same night and catch up afterward."

"Fantastic idea."

Ladd chattered about Aiden's return the entire time they worked to unload the trailer. His enthusiastic regard for Aiden was a testament to his impact on young people. While he enjoyed creating curricula and doing research, his priority was pouring wisdom and encouragement into his students. He cared about them, and it showed in their response to him.

As the last of the boxes were placed in the storage closet, Raven turned to him. "Ladd, do you know anything about students paying bribes in exchange for grades?"

He quickly straightened. "I've heard rumors. How did you find out about it?" His eyes rounded. "You don't think Dr. Ferrer is involved, do you? Because I can tell you right now, he'd never do something like that. He's honorable to the core. He expects his students to apply themselves and put forth their best effort."

Aiden appeared in the doorway. "Help. The aunts have served up their third piece of cake." He rubbed his midsection. "I can't eat another bite. You two need to come eat your share."

Ladd laughed. "Happy to do it."

They didn't linger over the cake and coffee the twins plied them with. They had a flash drive to find. With the evidence Aiden had compiled, they could end this tonight. And then she and Aiden could go their separate ways—for good this time.

* * *

As Raven turned into the paved drive attached to his parents' restored Craftsman, Aiden's chest felt tight. The night's emotional roller coaster wasn't ready to let him disembark quite yet. Seeing the twins and Ladd, being at Helping Hands, had been bittersweet. He wasn't sure when or if he'd get to be involved with that ministry again.

This part of the night would be even tougher. He'd wondered if he would ever see his childhood home again. The neighborhood was safe, nice and quiet, the kind with sidewalks, old-growth oaks and large yards for kids to play in. He'd been blessed with a carefree childhood, something Raven couldn't relate to.

She turned off the truck, the nostalgic tunes cutting off abruptly into silence, and wilted into the seat. He studied her profile while she stared at the house. The lightness in her mood had been snuffed out. That she wasn't thrilled to be here was obvious in her taut jaw, compressed lips, furrowed brow. The last time he'd seen her before disappearing had been here, the night of his father's retirement party.

"I remember the dress you wore that night," he said without preamble, knowing her thoughts were probably aligned with his. "It was a shimmery color, a blend of rose and gold that matched your eyes." They'd been like mysterious twin flames that night, concealing her thoughts from him. "Your hair was coiled at the nape of your neck. You wore swingy golden earrings that danced whenever you turned your head. You'd gotten a manicure…a French or Italian something, you called it, and you wore a flavored gloss on your lips. You made it impossible for me to concentrate. I could hardly make sensible conversation with the guests."

He'd been reminded how blessed he was to have her in his life—a beautiful, brave, brilliant woman devoted to others.

She fisted her hands on her lap. "The dress is hanging in my closet. I couldn't bring myself to part with it, because I was wearing it when we were last together. And because you admired it."

"I admired you in it, Raven. There's a difference." His voice was like gravel. "I've relived that night hundreds of times, you know. Trying to figure out what went wrong. While a swanky party at my parents' wasn't exactly your cup of tea, you were in a good mood at the start. Then something upset you. Something bad enough to end our engagement."

She said nothing. Was she replaying their argument? How it had started on the porch and spilled onto the steps and yard? He'd trailed her to the mailbox, frustrated and confused by her 180-degree mood shift, and begged her to explain. He'd been quaking in his polished loafers, aware he was losing her but unable to pinpoint why.

"Raven, tell me what happened."

Her throat convulsed, and she popped the door handle. "Let's focus on the case, all right?"

She was out of the car and striding toward the front door before he could utter another word. Last night at the stables, they'd worked out a plan. Aiden's parents would ask their next-door neighbor to leave the spare key under the mat for their friend, Raven. There was no reason to tell Mrs. Wilson or any of the other neighbors about Aiden at this point. News like that would be too big to contain.

She retrieved the key, entered first and turned on the overhead light. At her gasp, Aiden immediately pulled his weapon and moved to her side. His stomach dropped to his toes. Dirt and debris littered the entryway. A stained glass lamp had been knocked to the floor, and shards formed a broken rainbow against the hardwood.

He followed the trail of destruction to the living room on the left. The space looked as if a pack of wild dogs had been let loose in it—couch cushions shredded, floor lamp shoved over, plants overturned with dirt spilling out, curtains ripped from the windows. His mother's china cabinet hadn't been spared. The glass panes had been broken, and the delicate teapots and dishes were toppled. Books had been ripped from the built-ins and tossed in haphazard heaps.

He jerked in surprise when Raven touched his back. Her eyes issued a warning.

"Intruder could still be here," she murmured, easing the Glock from her waistband. "We have to do a sweep. Remember, don't touch anything. We'll have a team come out and search for trace evidence."

"Got it." Together, they checked every room on the first and second floors. The destruction was centered in the main areas, but the intruder had left his mark on the bedrooms and bathrooms, as well. Outrage burned in his gut.

At the basement stairs, Raven met his gaze. "Ready?"

She took the lead, weapon cradled in both hands, braced for potential danger. The finished basement consisted of a series of rooms—his mom's scrapbooking area, guest bedrooms, hang-out space and his dad's woodworking shop. They moved through them as swiftly and silently as they could. When she was satisfied they were alone, she holstered her weapon.

"I'm going to update the guys." Head bent, she texted Silver and Cruz. Their responses were almost instantaneous. "Desmond and Leonard haven't ventured out."

"They could've come yesterday. Before or in between classes. Or anytime between our meeting at the diner on Sunday and now."

"Assuming this wasn't a random burglary, how would the suspects know you collected evidence and what to look for?"

"I told Jay."

"And you think they elicited that information from him before staging his murder to look like an accidental drowning."

"I do."

She surveyed the space. "I'm going to see if your mom has some plastic gloves in the kitchen. We'll go through your things and then summon Morganton PD."

Aiden's belongings had been placed in clear plastic bins and stored in the guest room closest to his mom's craft room. The bins had been opened and the contents dumped on the carpet. His throat closed as he surveyed what was left of his former home—the one he'd purchased after earning his master's. He'd loved that old fifties bungalow. He'd bought it because it had good bones and would benefit from an overhaul. So much of his work and career required mental energy, and he liked the physical work of remodeling.

A broken picture frame caught his eye, and he bent to get a closer look. His PhD diploma. All that hard work, years of strenuous study capped with a dissertation… Had it been for nothing? Would he ever teach again? Once the truth came out, Abbott-Craig probably wouldn't be too pleased with his role in the school's reputation implosion that would follow. Would anyone want to hire a whistleblower?

"Found some." Raven reentered the room and held out a pair of disposable gloves. She'd already donned a pair. After a full day of activity, including hours in the saddle performing routine patrol, her braid was no longer tidy. Wisps skimmed her cheeks. "Let's sift through this stuff and place items in a box as we go."

He pulled on the gloves and picked up the frame. "We're looking for my record player."

"It was a tan color, right?" Her gaze was troubled, sad.

"Right."

They'd shared a love of music, specifically from the eighties, and they'd spent many evenings listening to records and playing dominoes. On Sunday afternoons after church, they'd sometimes browse thrift stores for old records.

During the search, her breath caught several times, and he knew she'd landed on yet another item attached to a memory. He gritted his teeth. He could relate—this place was an emotional minefield.

The record player wasn't among the items, however.

"The intruder could've found what he wanted and taken it."

Her knees rooted in the thick carpet, she braced her hands on her legs and contemplated their next move. "Let's go back through these rooms, then search again upstairs if we don't find it."

He trailed behind her as they retraced their steps. The woodworking area in the far corner of the basement had two exits, one regular and the other a garage door. The tools and equipment had barely been touched. A second look in the corner by the jigsaw told him why. Aiden's records had been stacked atop a metal shelf. On the cement below it, his record player lay in pieces.

Raven came up beside him, somber and silent. "Your dad must've brought it in here to listen to while he worked. A reminder of you."

In that moment, Aiden would've given anything to be able to hug his dad. He was tempted to get in his vehicle, drive to Florida and spend time with his parents before something truly tragic happened.

Instead, he crouched and sifted through the remains. Defeat sighed out of him. "The drive is gone."

Leonard and Desmond wouldn't hold on to the

evidence. They'd review it to see exactly what he knew and then destroy it. If he couldn't locate the other drive and prove they had motive to silence Jay, they may very well get away with their crimes. And then Jay's death would've been in vain.

Raven wanted out of this house. From the moment they'd pulled into the driveway, her spirit had felt heavy. This was where her and Aiden's dreams had died. The party had been a celebration of Francis's retirement. He'd taught high school science, and the house had been full of teachers, school board members and administrators. That in itself had put a wobble in her step. Odd that she could chase down criminals with fewer nerves than she possessed when mingling with educators. Childhood lessons ran deep.

Why can't you read? Are you lazy? You're simply not applying yourself, Raven. You have to work hard to achieve your greatest potential. Look at that writing! Looks like a kindergartner's.

She tried to push the buzzing thoughts from her mind by imagining a serene scene. A meadow with lush green grass, wildflowers and a bubbling stream. Thorn was there, grazing happily, his tail flicking back and forth.

Those days were long gone, those people out of her life.

But you're still listening to them, aren't you? Letting their judgment direct your decisions like a bit in a horse's mouth.

Being on Aiden's arm that night had stabilized her. Early in their relationship, she'd outlined her struggles, holding nothing back—giving him an out. He'd been wonderfully supportive. Admiring, even, of her accomplishments. He was proud of her work with the mounted police and extolled her virtues often. And even though his parents hadn't been as accepting, she'd thought it didn't matter.

Raven could still hear Helen disparaging Aiden's decision to marry her. Helen's friends had shared her concerns. Why would a brilliant professor marry someone with learning challenges? What if it was possible for her to pass on her deficits to their children?

She ground her teeth together. That last one had stung.

Aiden removed the gloves and crumpled them in one hand. "Once the police are done here, I'll have to clean up the mess. I don't want my parents to return and find their house in shambles."

"We'll all pitch in." Her focus returned to their present predicament—a lack of evidence to back up Aiden's claims of cheating within the university. Without it, the Morganton PD was unlikely to reopen Jay's case. "Let's go."

She was running on fumes. The past few days had been the hardest she'd lived through since those first days after Aiden's accident. This case had only begun, and she had a sneaking suspicion that getting enough evidence to convict these people was going to be tough.

The gray truck used as a getaway vehicle by Sunday night's shooter had been traced to its original owner, who'd reported it stolen hours before the incident. Cruz had personally driven to the diner where Aiden had met with Desmond. There were no security cameras, and the employees weren't willing to cooperate. Her neighbors hadn't caught anything useful on their cameras, either.

As for yesterday's courthouse shooting, they'd yet to find anything helpful in the video footage or photographs. Their hunch that Leonard was involved was a good one. This morning, after caring for the horses, they'd joined Officers Bell and Weiland and searched the woods again. Knowing Leonard's background narrowed their search and helped them construct a possible pattern of his movements. In all likelihood, he'd camouflaged himself using leaves and other natural material.

After firing at Aiden, he would've found a place to hide in plain sight. That theory had led them to a shallow creek that ran from the road beside the library and onto the farmer's property. They'd found a single boot print in the soft earth, and the soil had been disturbed, as if someone had lain prone there for some time. They hadn't found the casings, which meant he'd taken them with him. But the scene hadn't been protected, so even if the boot print could be linked to Leonard, it wouldn't be permissible in court. Amid all that dreary news was one blessing—Mitch was expected to fully recover.

At the top of the stairs, Raven encountered a closed door. She twisted the knob and anchored her foot on the top tread. The back of her neck prickled.

The kitchen was dark, and she knew for a fact they'd left the light on.

She reached for her gun, felt a hot breath on her neck, and something hard slammed into her skull. Bursts of light floated in her vision, and her knees refused to support her. She reached for the counter, determined to pull herself up. A boot landed square in her back with enough energy to force her onto her stomach. Out of breath and stunned from the pain, Raven twisted onto her side and saw the glint of a gun fitted with a silencer.

"No!" Aiden tackled the man as he pulled the

trigger, and the blast flashed orange in the dark. The shot went wide.

The pair tumbled to the tile and slammed into the stove. Aiden had a tight grip on the assailant's wrist and was trying to separate him from his weapon.

Raven clawed her way to standing and felt her stomach lurch. Ignoring the unsettling sensation and the throbbing inside her head, she reached for the light switch.

The light flooding the room seemed to startle the man. His face was concealed with a ski mask, and he was wearing gloves.

Aiden gained the upper position and smashed the man's hand against the tile. The gun slipped from his grasp. Raven kicked it out of the way. With a growl, the man lurched and bucked, dislodging Aiden and landing an elbow to his midsection. A groan indicated he'd hit the area where the bullet had left Aiden's chest bruised and sore.

Before she could assist Aiden, the intruder sprinted out the back entrance. She started after him, but a wave of dizziness quickly washed over her, and she slumped against the counter.

Aiden was at her side in an instant, one hand on her waist and the other on her shoulder, steadying her.

"I have to go after him," she said, her conviction strong but her body uncooperative.

"You're in no condition. Call in assistance."

He stayed close while Raven called Dispatch, who put officers in their vicinity on the perp's trail.

"Who was that, Aiden?"

"He had dark brown eyes. That's all I saw."

Had Leonard and Desmond figured out they were being watched and sent their cohort to finish them off? But how did they know their location?

Raven had underestimated their desperation to protect their interests. They didn't care who they hurt, or how many people.

Lawbreakers with everything to lose were the worst. Reckless and unpredictable. To top it off, she had no idea how many university faculty members were involved and how many were willing to spill blood.

EIGHT

Raven sank onto the corner of her bed. After working her braid loose with her fingers, she started to pull the brush through her hair. Her arms and upper back were sore from the intruder's rough handling. Lindsey noticed her frown and held out her hand.

"Here."

Raven hesitated.

"I'll be gentle, I promise."

She handed over the brush and shifted to give her friend better access. As promised, Lindsey had a light touch. The strain in her shoulders gradually eased.

Lindsey's cherry red Mini Cooper had been in her driveway when they returned from Morganton. Silver had told her what happened, and she'd come to see for herself that Raven was okay. And to provide moral support. None of Raven's other friends knew what was going on. Nor could they begin to understand the strain she was under.

Lindsey, on the other hand, had intimate knowledge of danger. It was what had forced her and Silver to acknowledge their relationship went far beyond professional. Now they were about to get married.

The men's voices filtered in from the kitchen, but she couldn't make out their words. No doubt her partners were grilling Aiden. They'd converged here after Raven and Aiden had met with the patrol officers who'd responded to her call.

She studied her reflection in the closet door mirror. Carefully probing her bruised jaw, she said, "This will fade before the wedding. Makeup will take care of the rest."

There was a chipped nail, too. Raven would need the manicure Lindsey had scheduled for the bridal party this weekend.

Behind her red-framed glasses, Lindsey's big brown eyes were soft with compassion. "Bruises don't matter to me. I just want you there in one piece."

Raven lifted her chin and tried to project confidence. "I *will* be there."

Lindsey's smile didn't have the bright, movie theater wattage it usually did. "I know the four of you have plenty of training and experience, but that doesn't mean I don't worry about you all. I try not to dwell on what *could* happen. I have to pray about it a lot. Every day, actually. Some days, every hour."

Loving a law enforcement officer presented unique challenges. Their jobs were stressful and always carried a measure of risk. Even a routine traffic stop could go upside down. Yet she'd never thought she'd have to worry about Aiden's profession. How wrong she'd been.

"We have to trust in God's plan and protection." She pointed to the decorative canvas print beside the window that showcased one of her favorite verses.

But without faith it is impossible to please Him, for he that cometh to God must believe that He is, and that He is a rewarder of them that diligently seek Him.

"I repeat that one over and over to myself." She reached over her shoulder and squeezed Lindsey's arm. "I'm glad you came over."

She snorted. "Silver isn't."

"He doesn't want you anywhere near this case. After everything you two went through, I don't blame him."

Silver had almost come apart at the seams when Lindsey's life was threatened in the weeks before Christmas. By the time they caught the perpetrator, he'd realized he couldn't live without her.

"You didn't abandon me when I was in trouble," she said, waving the brush for emphasis. "I'm not about to abandon you."

The hall floorboards creaked, and Silver appeared in the doorway. His styled hair had lost some of its starch, and his eyes were bloodshot.

Why did this have to happen now, Lord? Less than two weeks before their special day?

They should be spending their free time anticipating their new life together. There were a million and one things for the bride to accomplish, and as a bridesmaid, Raven was supposed to provide support.

"My buddy over at Morganton PD sent over the file on Jay," he said. "Care to pull it up on your laptop?"

Raven retrieved her computer from the study she'd set up in one of the spare bedrooms. Lindsey, no doubt to give them privacy, retreated to her bedroom to finish packing items she'd left behind. In the kitchen, Cruz and Silver had taken seats at the table. Aiden stood at the door, peering through the blinds. He reminded her of a brooding sentinel, always keeping watch.

"You shouldn't be at the window," she stated, her voice sterner than she'd intended.

He pivoted toward her, his gaze intense as he

took in her unbound hair and her bruised and tender cheek. His curls were disheveled, his jaw shadowed with scruff and his features stamped with fatigue. He was the most striking man she'd ever set eyes on, and he still had the power to make her knees weak.

Aiden folded his arms over his chest and thought better of it. Dropped them back to his sides. They'd both refused medical treatment at the scene. That blow to his chest had surely exacerbated the deep bruising he'd gotten from the gunshot. There was a tear in his long-sleeved, sea blue shirt with a Louisiana boat tour emblem. At the rate he was going through clothes, he'd need replacements soon.

She opened the silverware drawer and gestured to the bottle of pain reliever. "This is here if you need it."

He thanked her and stationed himself at the opposite end of the table. She slid her laptop over to Silver, who brought up the file and read the scant details aloud.

"That's it?" Aiden gripped the chair, his knuckles going white.

Silver lifted his gaze. "The responding officers cataloged the scene and deemed it an accidental drowning. They had no reason to suspect foul play."

"But it wasn't an accident," he asserted.

"Wouldn't they have at least spoken to his family and friends? Asked if he drank and how often?"

"Not if they were short on manpower." Silver shifted in his chair. "You have to remember, the drowning happened in a neighborhood comprised mostly of college students. You're aware of the stereotype. College kids take risks. They experiment, sometimes to their detriment."

"Jay wasn't like that." Sadness pulled at the corners of his mouth. She wanted to wrap her arms around him and never let go. He blamed himself for the young man's death, and that was a heavy burden to shoulder.

Raven moved closer but stopped short of touching him. "We'll start with the person who called it in and work from there. We'll knock on apartment doors. Someone may have seen something but was too scared to approach the police."

"They have to pay for what they did." His eyes begged for promises she couldn't make.

"We're going to work to find evidence that will stand up in the court of law. That's the only guarantee I can give you."

Aiden eased the curtain aside but couldn't distinguish any specific features of Raven's backyard, let alone discern if someone was out there. He'd given up on sleep. His mind wouldn't rest. *Lord, please don't let Jay's murder go unpun-*

ished. Please don't let anyone else die because of my quest for truth.

"You don't have to keep watch, you know."

He hadn't heard Raven stir since bidding her good-night an hour ago. Letting the curtain fall into place, he turned toward the hallway. She looked comfortable in her cable-knit sweater thrown over a T-shirt and leggings. Socks with horses on them kept her feet warm.

"The patrol officer is stationed outside," she said, bunching the lapels of her sweater together. "You need rest."

"My body knows that, but…" He shrugged. "Did I disturb you?"

"My thoughts are like horses at a racetrack." Her gaze surveyed the bedding on the couch, the rumpled pillow and blankets. "Want some steamed milk?"

She declined his help, so he returned to his position by the French doors. He gritted his teeth until his jaw ached. He yearned to be near her, to cuddle on the couch like they used to, warm mugs in hand while they watched the flames dance in the fireplace.

He rested his forehead against the doorframe and closed his eyes. *This is harder than I ever imagined, Lord. When I dreamed about seeing her again, I failed to factor in the turmoil of knowing she no longer wants a future with me.*

The man he'd been before had been positioned to win her back. He could've fought to overcome her reservations. But that was no longer an option.

"Here you go." Raven set his mug on the coffee table and noticed the oversize book lying open.

"It was on the shelf," he said, picking up his mug and taking a sip of the frothy milk. She'd added vanilla syrup like she used to. "I didn't think you'd mind."

She settled on the far end of the couch, tucked her legs to one side and cupped her mug between her hands. Her hair spilled over her shoulders in inky streams. The bruises on her jaw had deepened to an angry purple mixed with green. She claimed it looked worse than it felt.

"I haven't taken out the art books since your accident, but I couldn't bring myself to donate them."

He sat down, leaving ample space between them, then pulled the book onto his lap and contemplated the colorful pictures. "Remember the first time I took you to Atlanta?"

"The High Museum. I didn't expect to enjoy it."

Raven had introduced him to the world of horses. He, in turn, had wanted to share his love of fine art. Since she tended to think in pictures, he'd suspected she would enjoy viewing paintings and sculptures. That first day at the High, she'd made quips about what was going on in the paintings. She'd made up stories. He'd joined her, and they'd stayed until closing. After that, he'd bought her art appreciation books. They'd continued their silly game and sometimes competed to see who could make up the best story.

Remembering the fun and closeness they'd once shared, he flipped the page and angled it toward her. "What's going on in this one?"

She stared at the photograph until her eyes got shiny. Then, her throat working, she set her mug aside and sprang off the couch. "I can't."

"Why not?"

"Because you died! Because I hadn't yet come to terms with our broken engagement before I got the phone call no one ever wants. Your car veered off the road and sank beneath the surface. They couldn't find your body. I had hope, you know. For days, I hoped. Begged God." She flung out her hands. "Played that story game with your accident. Maybe you managed to get free, but you hit your head and lost your memories. Someone found you, but you couldn't remember your name. Maybe you were disoriented and got lost. It was in the low thirties that night. You were soaked. Hypothermia could've set in. I had all these thoughts running through my mind…" Her voice broke, and she buried her face in her hands.

Aiden couldn't stay away. He approached her as he would a skittish horse, ready to back off if she gave the signal. He wrapped his arms around her. She didn't yield, didn't bend. As the moments passed, her resistance faded. She melted into him, her face flush against his chest, and latched on to his belt loops. Sobs worked their way up and spilled out. It made him think she'd never allowed herself to mourn the end of their relationship.

The fissures in his heart yawned wider. "I'm so very sorry. I panicked that night and made a split-second decision. Once on that path, I couldn't figure out how to course correct." He was a planner by nature. When confronted with a problem or decision, he considered various avenues and their ramifications. He made pros and cons lists. Rush judgments were never ideal, but with Raven's life in jeopardy, he'd had to act fast.

The top of her head came even with his nose. He pressed his cheek to her temple and stroked her hair. A sense of rightness filled him, making those long, lonely days and nights fade from memory. He'd disappeared because of her. He'd returned because of her. Everything came back to Raven. She was his joy, his partner, his sounding board.

She's not yours anymore. She stopped being yours the day she returned your ring.

When her tears were spent and she stepped out of his arms, swiping at her cheeks and keeping her gaze averted, he let his arms fall to his sides.

"Can you forgive me?"

She lifted her watery, reddened gaze to his. "I'm hurt and angry, Aiden. I don't approve of how you handled this whole thing. But I know that causing me pain would never be your first choice."

"Is that a yes?" He needed to know for sure.

"Yes, I forgive you."

He had no time to bask in those words. Her phone chimed an alert, and her expression altered as she read the text.

"We have an in injured camper inside the national park. The SAR team needs our assistance extracting him. I have to go." She strode down the hall, tossing over her shoulder, "The patrol officer will stay and guard you."

Aiden didn't love the idea of being separated from her. If he had his wish, he wouldn't let her out of his sight again. When the officer knocked on the door and told them he had to respond to a domestic violence call, Aiden wasn't disappointed.

"I'll come with you," he told Raven.

At her doubtful look, he said, "I haven't forgotten how to ride. I had the best teacher, remember?"

She looked startled at being referred to as a teacher, and it made him sad. Her poor experiences had shaped her self-image and had played a significant role in their relationship's demise.

"You're up to being in the saddle in the cold, dark mountains for a few hours?"

"I am."

Anything to stay close to her, no matter how detrimental that was to his heart.

NINE

At the staging area, Raven's plans to have Aiden accompany them were thwarted. Lieutenant Hatmaker saw him astride King and immediately intervened. Aiden wasn't a trained volunteer and would be a liability. She didn't try to change his mind. Hatmaker was notoriously stubborn. Besides, he had a point.

A light mist began to coat everything in sight. She retrieved her poncho from the truck and put it on over her uniform. Grabbing an extra one, she made her way to the tent canopy where the rescue was being organized. Portable lights on tripods had been placed around the perimeter. Law enforcement and SAR team vehicles lined either side of the dirt access road. Aiden stood on the group's fringe, listening to the discussion but not participating actively.

He noticed her approach and met her halfway. "Thanks."

As he slipped the poncho over his head, Raven's tears threatened again. She had buried her grief deep in order to soldier through the memorial and, later, to help his parents decide what to keep of his belongings and what to sell or donate. Afterward, it had been easier to continue on that way. Holding it in. Controlling it, instead of letting it control her. Tonight, she'd been too weary to contain it.

Aiden had given her a safe space to release the pent-up emotion tied to everything she'd gone through this past year.

From the start, Aiden had been a safe space for her. He was the kind of person to invite confidences. Nonjudgmental. Attentive. Supportive. It was part of why she'd fallen in love with him. Her mom had picked a variety of rotten apples as boyfriends, many of them with nasty tempers. Aiden was patient, laid-back and rarely got riled up—all major points in his favor.

She blinked away the tears before his head cleared the poncho's opening. Enough with the crying. He'd apologized, and she'd forgiven him. They could move on with their lives and finally begin the healing process. As soon as they had this case wrapped up, they'd go their separate ways.

Silver and Cruz rode into her sight line on their respective mounts. Their helmets gleamed in the artificial light.

Silver's brows lifted. "Ready?"

She held up her hand to indicate she'd be a minute.

"Stay close to the command team, okay?"

Aiden's jaw was tight, his expression grave. "I'll be right here when you get back."

Raven returned to the horse trailer, untied Thorn and climbed into the saddle. She prayed before every patrol and mission, aware she couldn't perform her duties without God's help. She liked the verses that spoke of Jesus as the vine and believers as branches. The image was clear in her mind, and it helped her remember the core truth. To accomplish anything of value, to do God's will, she had to rely on Him.

I'm going to need an extra dose of strength tonight, Lord. I'm tired, emotionally spent and unhappy about leaving Aiden behind. Please help me focus and be an asset to this team effort. Keep us safe.

The rescue operation took them several miles into the national park. With each mile, Raven's worries flared. She had to remind herself time and again that God loved Aiden and had a plan for him. He'd protected him all this time. As seriously as she took her role of protector, she didn't have the ultimate say in what happened. God did.

The path widened, and Cruz guided Renegade

to her side. The light from his headlamp cast his face in alternating shadows.

"You're quiet."

"I'm just trying to get through the next hour, Cruz." And the hour after that.

When Cruz Castillo had first joined their unit, Raven hadn't liked him. His passionate personality was too reminiscent of her mother's boyfriends. But as they worked together, she saw that he cared deeply about the citizens they'd sworn to protect. He admitted that he had to work extra hard at bridling his reactions—injustice constantly gnawed at his sense of right and wrong. She, in turn, had confided in him that she had to work extra hard to manage her dyslexia. Their bond had grown, and she'd come to treasure his friendship.

"Is the professor pressuring you to get back with him? If so, the two of us can have a chat."

"What? No. That's not his style. Why do you assume he wants that, anyway?"

While Aiden clearly cared about her safety, he hadn't mentioned repairing their relationship.

"It's obvious."

"That won't stand up in court, Officer," she retorted.

"I know what I know." He shrugged. "Why'd you break up?"

"I can't talk about this now."

She didn't want to hear Cruz's strong opinions about her reasons. They would seem inconsequential to him. Easily overcome. He wouldn't understand.

He didn't press her. They rode in silence through the hushed woods. Thankfully, the clouds didn't open up on them. They were able to reach the camper's backcountry site without any issues. The injured man's wife led them to the spot where he'd slipped into a ravine and broken his leg. Their unit worked with the SAR team to secure the patient and extract him using a travois. The entire operation took most of the night, but they were able to deliver the patient to the staging area and waiting ambulance. By that time, Raven was close to falling out of the saddle from exhaustion.

The sky overhead was creeping toward dawn, the deep black shifting to soft purple. She longed for rest, but they had to drive to the stables first and see to the horses' needs. The sight of Aiden woke her right up, as if she'd chugged an energy drink. He stood talking with one of the park rangers near the canopy. Safe and sound.

She nudged Thorn in their direction. A relieved smile transformed Aiden's features, and he started toward her. Suddenly the report of a rifle echoed through the coves, startling her. Thorn's muscles quivered, awaiting her orders.

The park ranger snagged Aiden's arm before he could rush in her direction. Raven yelled for them to take cover. Her words were drowned out by another shot, this one busting out the windshield of the vehicle the men were crouched beside. She withdrew her 9mm, guided Thorn to the vehicle and, acting as a shield, waited impatiently for Aiden and the ranger to move around to the trunk and hunker down. Her instincts were to ride straight for the shooter's location. Over the radio, Silver and Cruz ordered her to stay put while they rooted him out.

One of the SAR team members rushed over, and Raven directed her to join the men. She and Thorn edged backward until they, too, could use the vehicle as cover.

Seconds after they got into place, someone fired from the woods behind them, this time at close range. A tire popped from the impact. They were being ambushed from both sides.

Aiden shifted his body so that the rescue team member wasn't in the line of fire. The park ranger boxed her in from the other side. They had the disadvantage. The second shooter wasn't visible in the woods, but he could see them thanks to the spotlights.

Raven's radio was abuzz with communication. Not surprisingly, she stayed in the saddle.

She and Thorn were a team. Most of her duties could be performed from her perch. In this case, it made her a target. He clamped his mouth shut to stop the complaints from erupting. He couldn't tell her how to do her job. She and Thorn whirled around and, her body and focus fixed on the woods, instructed the three of them to inch around the sedan and get between it and the truck parked nearby. She ordered them to stay close to the side and make themselves as small as possible.

The park ranger went first, then the woman and Aiden. His heart rate thrummed in his ears. *Please, God, protect us all. Bring these men into captivity tonight.*

Another bullet whizzed through the air. Raven cried out, and Aiden sprang out of his protected position.

"Raven!"

Her Glock in her right hand, she gripped her upper arm with her left. Her face was bleached of color.

"I'm fine. Stay here. I'm going to find this guy." She gave Thorn the command and, together, they charged into the woods.

Staying behind while she chased down the shooter was almost as hard as disappearing the night of the accident had been. She was hurt. Exhausted.

* * *

Before he resumed his spot on the hard-packed earth, another gunshot cracked through the cove. Reason deserted him. He dashed into the woods after her and unsheathed his gun. He paused to let his eyes adjust and listen for clues. Good thing he had on dark clothes and could blend into the environment. He headed in the direction he heard movement, careful where he stepped, his muscles trembling with tension.

The deeper he went without crossing paths with Raven or the shooter, the louder his doubts shouted. If he became lost, he'd create more work for the mounted police unit. What had he been thinking, anyway? How was he supposed to protect her like this?

Just as Aiden pivoted, intent on returning to the staging area, the blow came seemingly from out of nowhere. Lights exploded in his vision as needles of pain pierced his skull. His stomach lurched. He hit his knees as the darkness deepened around him. At first, he thought it was impending unconsciousness. Then he realized fabric had been draped over his face and pulled tight. As he fought to breathe, he dropped his gun and clawed at the thick, scratchy material.

He'd made a terrible mistake.

TEN

Raven's wound burned. It had started to drizzle, and the raindrops were like icicles pricking her face. Frustration gnawed at her. She'd gotten close to the shooter a couple of times, had heard him running away, his footsteps crunching against a thick layer of old leaves and his body brushing against trees, snapping off brittle branches. But he'd remained just out of reach.

She tugged on the reins to stop Thorn again. Every few yards she did this—listened and assessed. This time, she heard what sounded like a moan and an ensuing struggle. Using her high-powered flashlight, she forged ahead, her gaze swinging from left to right, following the beam's arc.

It caught on the silhouettes of two men—one standing behind the other, who was on his knees and trying to get free of the sweater wrapped around his face.

"Freeze! Let me see your hands."

The masked aggressor's head jerked up, and he took off. The other man tossed the material to the ground and, sucking in lungfuls of air, clambered to his feet. He spun around, eyes squinting in the bright light, and Raven's stomach dropped to her boots.

"Aiden!" Thorn reacted to her nonverbal commands and brought her swiftly to his side. She holstered her weapon and reached out a gloved hand. "Are you all right?"

He grasped her hand and squeezed it. "Your timing is impeccable," he said raggedly.

"Why aren't you with the ranger? Why did you disregard my instructions? You could've been killed." Her lungs deflated. "For real, this time."

"You don't know what it's like to watch someone you care about put herself in danger," he said grimly, shoulders squaring. "Danger you led straight to her."

He probed a spot on his head and grimaced. The pain was written clearly all over his face.

"What's wrong?"

"He whacked me over the head. How's your arm?"

"Pretty sure it's a surface wound. Are you dizzy? Vision blurry?"

"No to both."

"Let's rejoin the others. We'll discuss your reluctance to follow police orders later."

His sigh seemed to be pried from deep within, and she regretted the barb. How would she feel if their roles were reversed? She couldn't be sure she would have a different reaction.

Back at the staging area, Cruz and Silver had returned empty-handed. The sheriff's department had responded to the call, as this part of the national park fell under their jurisdiction. A deputy was interviewing the witnesses.

Cruz's piercing gaze bounced between them. "What happened out there?"

Aiden jerked a thumb toward her. "She's been shot and needs attention."

Silver had already dismounted Lightning and was about to load him in the trailer.

"Where?"

"My arm." Raven slid out of the saddle and found herself surrounded by three overly concerned males. "It's a graze, that's all."

Before her partners could act, Aiden invaded her space, nudged her into the light and carefully peeled the layer of torn sleeves aside. His fingers were cold but gentle on the sensitive flesh around the wound.

He dragged his gaze to hers. "Your first aid kit should do the trick."

"What about you?"

"I didn't lose consciousness."

"You could have a concussion."

"Do either of you need medical attention?" Cruz asked.

They both shook their heads.

"Then I'd like an explanation."

Aiden outlined the events. Her blood ran cold when he got to the confrontation with the perp.

Raven held up the jacket Aiden had recovered. "This belonged to the shooter we encountered. Maybe we'll find trace evidence or a clue as to where he bought it. I'm sure he left some other markers behind in the woods. He was sloppy."

Cruz placed the jacket in an evidence bag. "Think he could be the same guy who accosted you at the Ferrers?"

She looked at Aiden, who shrugged. "I couldn't say."

The gun left by that intruder was still being examined, but they'd learned the serial number had been filed off.

"Our guy was a ghost," Silver said. "But it's worth having a look around in the daylight. We might find a casing. The sheriff's department will let us know what they find. For now, we've got to get these horses loaded and returned to the stables."

The ride took place in almost total silence. By the time they got there, the sun had lifted above the mountain peaks, the rays cutting through the mist hovering above the ground. Silver and

Cruz insisted on caring for the horses. When she emerged from the locker room in a fresh set of clothes, Aiden was waiting on her.

He searched her face. "All good?"

"Cleaned, medicated and bandaged." All she needed now was several hours of uninterrupted sleep.

"Have you been shot before?"

Unable to bear the self-recrimination in his eyes, she framed his face in her hands. His lips parted, and he sucked in a swift breath. "Hear me now, Aiden Ferrer. You didn't pull that trigger. You aren't the villain here. What happens to me is because of someone else's actions. Got it?"

He swallowed hard. "I'm worried about you."

Raven got lost in his molten brown eyes. She scraped her thumbs over his bristled jaw. Let her fingers tangle in his curls. His hands found her hips, and he squeezed his eyes shut.

"Raven." His voice was both a plea and a warning.

The magnetic pull that had always hovered beneath the surface, ready to snap them together, exerted its power. She gazed at his mouth. What would it hurt to share one kiss? For old time's sake?

Aiden was alive and well, not a figment of her imagination, not a figure in her dreams. She'd missed him for so long, missed their connection.

What she'd shared with Aiden had been severed without warning, and her last memory of him had haunted her day and night—the confusion, the demand for answers, the pain she'd inflicted.

Raven lifted her face and touched her lips to his. A shudder worked its way through Aiden's body. His fingers bunched in her shirt fabric. In that moment, everything was right in her world. Good. Beautiful. *Glorious.*

"You guys ready for me to follow you home?" Cruz's voice shattered the illusion.

She stumbled back and pressed her fingers to her mouth, wishing she could bottle that moment and relive it again and again.

Aiden's eyes were turbulent. Was he angry? Hurt?

"Sorry. Didn't mean to intrude." Cruz hooked a thumb behind him. "I'll be in the parking lot." He beat a hasty retreat.

"I shouldn't have," she rushed out. "I didn't think."

Nothing had changed. Nothing ever would.

"We've had a long night," he said at last. "Let's forget it happened."

"You mean pretend it didn't happen?"

"Whatever works for you, Raven."

Raven had kissed him. A brief, tortuous, emotion-packed kiss that couldn't be forgotten.

He'd thought his heart had been broken before, but he suspected that by the time this ordeal was over, there'd be nothing left of the man he used to be. He wouldn't be able to come back from saying goodbye to her a second time. No more chances. No new love in the years to come. He'd found the woman of his dreams, the one he wanted by his side day in and day out, the one he wanted to raise his children. The problem? She couldn't envision a future with him. Even if her mindset changed, he had nothing to offer her.

That kiss had been spontaneous. She hadn't been in the right frame of mind to consider the ramifications. How could he blame her? They'd both been under significant stress since he'd dropped back into her life.

They hadn't discussed it during the brief ride to her house. This morning, there had been an increased tension between them. Thankfully, that had lessened throughout the day as they worked their way through the list of his former students and it became increasingly evident that convincing someone to admit wrongdoing would be more difficult than he'd realized. The students they'd visited hadn't responded to Raven's offer of a deal or appeals to common decency.

He and Raven entered the rock climbing center near campus. Built after his car accident, the center was advertised as the largest in the state.

"This is the last student on our list," she said, brushing her hair over her shoulder. She'd dressed in civilian clothes so as not to intimidate the students. Her rose sweater was buttoned over a shell pink shirt and paired with jeans and tan ankle boots. The soft hues enhanced her complexion and jet-black hair. "If he's as reluctant to help as the others, we'll have to go to plan B."

"Do you have a plan B?"

Her bow-shaped lips quirked. "I've got some ideas floating around in my head."

The customers ahead of them finished their transaction and continued past the counter. The young man working the register greeted them. "Can I help you folks?"

"We're looking for Zane Simon," Aiden said. "Is he working today?"

"Who's asking?"

Raven flashed a smile along with her badge. "Officer Hart. I'm with the Serenity Mounted Police."

His eyes rounding, he jerked a thumb over his shoulder. "He's in the bouldering area. It's past the children's climbing section and across from the restrooms."

"Thank you."

The ceilings were high, the floors carpeted and the climbing surfaces varying shades of primary colors.

"Nice addition to the town," Aiden remarked, observing the climbers as they passed. "Looks like a place you and I would've spent time in."

At her hasty side glance, he clamped his lips together.

She led the way into the bouldering area, where people climbed without the use of ropes. There were fewer people here, and only one who fit the age and physical description from a distance.

Raven tilted her head back and called up. "Zane Simon?"

The man peered over his shoulder. "He's outside."

"Can you point us in the general direction?"

"The exit you want is beside the gym on the upper level."

As they walked away, Aiden raised his brows. "They have a gym here?"

She shrugged. "I've heard great things about this place but haven't made time to visit."

The exit he'd specified was clearly marked. When they emerged onto a metal walkway bolted to the building's stucco exterior, they received a surprise. This section faced away from the street and was dotted with climbing handholds and footholds. Three climbers clung to the side like that famous superhero, not caring that it was early February, cloudy and cold enough to sting his ears.

He and Raven exchanged a look. Framing her mouth with her hands, she yelled up to the climbers. "Zane Simon?"

The two males climbing close together looked down. The one wearing a mustard-colored beanie lifted his hand.

"Be right there."

As they waited, Aiden surveyed the cars in the lot below. He couldn't let his guard down. Today was Wednesday, and Leonard and Desmond were at work. But the mounted unit had yet to uncover the third man's identity. He could follow them anywhere without them knowing—a dangerous advantage.

The walkway juddered with the thump of Zane's tennis shoes. Aiden's gaze swerved to the young man. He didn't recognize him. While his upper level classes had small numbers, the first-year classes had ranged between thirty and forty students.

"Can I help you?" Zane deftly unhooked from the ropes. His blue eyes were friendly and inquisitive beneath the knit cap. There was no indication he was an employee, other than his helpful demeanor. The guy at the counter hadn't worn a uniform, either.

Raven introduced herself and extended her hand toward him. "This is Dr. Aiden Ferrer."

Zane's nostrils flared, and his expression became less eager to please. "Did you want to sign up for a climbing class? Owen has flyers at the information desk."

"I think you know why we're here, Zane." Aiden crossed his arms and gave him a direct stare. "I taught at Abbott-Craig. You flunked my class, yet here you are a junior in the architecture program. How do you explain that?"

Zane's eyes darted to the left and right, as if searching for a way out.

"How many more classes did Leonard fix for you?" he pressed.

Real fear snaked over his face, and he edged backward. But the walkway extended only to the end of the building. He and Raven blocked the lone exit.

"I... I don't know what you're talking about."

Raven rested her hands on her hips. "Zane, we're not here to cause problems for you. We're here because we need your help."

"What do you want from me?"

"Leonard murdered a student named Jay Crowell," Aiden blurted. "A student who also slipped Leonard cash in exchange for altered grades. He has to be brought to justice."

Raven shot him a startled look. They hadn't told the others about Jay, thinking it would scare them into silence. None of them had agreed to help, anyway, so what did it matter? Zane was their last chance.

Zane blanched. He raised his palms. "I don't know anything about a murder, I promise."

"We believe you." Raven reassured him. "We need someone to agree to come forward about Leonard's cheating scheme. If we can prove he had motive, we can get Jay's case reopened."

He raised his arms, elbows flung out, and dug his fingertips into the back of his neck. He stared at the horizon. "I can't. I'd lose my scholarships. I'm enrolled in a study abroad mini semester this summer."

Aiden didn't add that Zane would likely get expelled. Or at the very least, lose credit for the classes Leonard fixed for him. He'd have to repeat them, and it wouldn't be for free.

"Like you, Jay had plans. Dreams. Family and friends. He was only twenty years old, and his life was cut short. For what? Because a greedy, ruthless man decided he was a threat. I saw his dead body, saw Leonard trying to make it look like an accident..." Aiden fisted his hands and spoke around the lump in his throat. "Leonard's trying to do the same thing to Raven and me. If you don't speak up, you're letting a murderer walk free."

Zane swayed a little on his feet.

Raven put her palms together in a pleading

gesture. "Listen to me, Zane—we can protect you. We can make sure you don't face criminal charges. All you have to do is talk to us. Give us dates. Details."

His lips almost disappeared as he considered his options. Aiden winged desperate prayers upward.

Without warning, Zane bolted, shoving between them and knocking Raven off-kilter as he passed. Aiden grabbed her arm, stabilizing her. The door slammed with finality.

He hoped he didn't look as defeated as he felt. "Now what?"

She huffed a grim sigh. "Plan B."

ELEVEN

Aiden thought Raven's plan B—to pose as a prospective student interested in athletic teams and gain the cooperation of an athlete—was a good one. However, he wanted to search for his other flash drive first. He'd taped it to a framed painting's rear panel hanging on his office wall. Although a long shot, there was a chance his replacement had liked the painting and decided to keep it. So instead of returning to Serenity after the rock climbing center disappointment, they'd hung around Morganton, staying out of sight until the majority of the university's classes ended.

Hunkered down in the passenger seat of her car, which was parked on the curb beside the university's central supply store, Aiden gobbled up the familiar sights—the football stadium, the student union where he'd met colleagues for lunch. Being back on campus brought a wave of longing and nostalgia. He'd spent the majority of his adult life on a college campus…five years of undergraduate study, followed by the pursuit of his master's and then PhD. He'd taught at Abbott-Craig for four years. This was his second home, and now it was one he'd essentially banished himself from, thanks to his amateur sleuthing.

A young woman on a bicycle whizzed past, backpack bouncing. The flow of students on the sidewalks had dwindled to a mere trickle. Most were probably in the cafeterias dotted about campus, enjoying supper with friends. Or in their dorm rooms, hunkering down for an evening of coursework. He'd missed the energy of campus life more than he'd realized.

His gaze passed over the vibrant window displays showcasing university gear in the school's signature purple. Raven emerged, bags in hand. Although her thirtieth birthday was coming up, she could pass for a young college student in her sweater, jeans and canvas sneakers. A light breeze teased her loose hair, tossing strands across her face. She brushed them behind her ear and hurried to the car.

Cold air hit him as she resumed her spot behind the wheel. He took the bags from her and glanced at the contents—purple caps and hoodies. "An art kit?"

"Thought I'd carry it. Blend in with the art students. They were having a BOGO half off sale."

She flashed him a smile that made his heart do somersaults.

"You used the cash I gave you?"

She averted her gaze and pulled onto the street. "I planned to put it back in your wallet when you weren't looking."

At least she was honest. "You think I wouldn't notice?"

"Aiden, it's a few items of clothing."

"What about the meals you've been feeding me? I refuse to be a burden to you."

"You're not."

"Raven."

"Fine, I'll keep the money."

"Thank you."

He directed her to the parking area beside the art and architecture building. At the sight of the concrete and glass structure, his breath caught in his throat. The rows of windows at the top of the building shone like pearls in a necklace. The curved glass panels that housed the fire stairways also emitted welcome light.

"Having second thoughts?" Raven asked. "It's unlikely that your flash drive is still inside."

"I have to make sure."

"All right. Let's do this."

He was grateful she hadn't tried to dissuade him. They pulled the hoodies on over their clothes and donned the caps, pulling them low over their faces. They'd chosen to come at this time because there were enough people in the building for them not to be conspicuous. Also, the doors locked at eleven, and they would need a student ID card to enter after that. There was usually an evening class in session, and students would be in the various bays working on projects. Undergrads from four different divisions used this building—art, architecture, landscape architecture and interior design.

His heart raced as they approached the side entrance, but not because of the threat. Because he couldn't wait to get inside. He itched to be part of this again...the learning, sharing ideas, molding minds, sparking creativity. He wanted to design, to contribute to the community in a meaningful way, to help people achieve their goals.

Raven tried the glass doors. "Locked."

"Right. I forgot these side entrances are locked after six. We'll have to use the south one."

They strode along the sidewalk and made a left, walking beneath the jutting portion of the building that created a breezeway, and entered near the bagel shop. Inside the atrium that reached to the ceiling four stories above their heads, Aiden was tempted to gawk like a tourist. He wanted to tilt his head back and take it all in again. The exposed mechanical systems painted muted green and yellow. The walkways, the office bays jutting out into the open central space, windows overlooking the atrium below.

He resisted the urge, knowing he could be easily recognized by anyone—bagel shop employee, maintenance man, faculty member, former student.

Raven looped her arm through his, making him aware he'd stopped dead in his tracks and forced a passerby to walk around him. "We're going upstairs, right?" she prompted. "Third floor?"

"Yes." He began walking at a casual pace, covering her hand with his. "Northeast corner."

They walked past the full-size trees and vacant café tables. As they passed the auditorium, the door swung open and students streamed out. Their professor was among them, a man who'd befriended Aiden in his early days on the job. Alarmed, Aiden ducked behind the nearest tree, bringing Raven with him.

He leaned in close and rested his hand in the curve of her neck and shoulder where the hoodie fabric bunched. Her eyes were wide with questions. Anyone looking would think they were having an intimate conversation.

"The man in the khakis and blue button-down? He knows me well."

Her gaze shifted beyond him. "He's stopped to chat with someone."

He grimaced.

She bit her lower lip. "This place hasn't changed, has it?"

"Not that I can see."

He'd been proud to show her around, giving her a tour of the building, showing her his office, introducing her to some of his students in the lab. She'd even sat in on one of his lectures. He could count on one hand the times she'd visited him after that.

"Look at their faces," she murmured now. "Excited to learn. Confident in themselves and their professor."

He tried not to be distracted by her nearness. Her lovely scent that made him think of fragrant apple orchards in spring. "That night at my parents' party."

Her gaze snapped back to his, and she stiffened.

"You said your learning disability would always be an obstacle between us."

"Yes."

"But you accepted my proposal. You were excited to plan the wedding ceremony. We discussed where to live—"

"Argued is more like it. We couldn't agree whether to live in Serenity or here."

That had been a sore spot. Silly, when he thought about it. He'd live in a barn if it meant being with Raven. "What made you reconsider? What happened at the party? Did someone say something to you?"

"This is hardly the time."

He'd struck a nerve. "Raven—"

"He's leaving." Drawing away from him, she grabbed his hand and tugged him toward the concrete stairway that appeared to float in the middle of the atrium.

Only she could scramble his thoughts. He'd actually forgotten where he was and why he was there for a minute. Together, they climbed the stairs to the third floor, keeping their faces pointed to their shoes. They strode past open studio spaces outfitted with desks and computers, past the print shop and photo lab, until they reached the offices opposite the woodshop.

His was in the corner, which had afforded him a fantastic view of campus and the mountains in the distance. The placard displayed someone else's name.

He removed the key from his pocket, grateful they'd found it among his belongings. He made quick work of the lock. Raven entered first, and he closed the door behind her and turned on the light. The new occupant had made changes. The desk was in a new spot, the walls were painted a garish green and potted plants crowded every available space.

Raven arched a brow but didn't comment. Aiden scanned the walls for his artwork and felt the hope seep out of him.

"It's not here."

Built-in shelves with cabinets on the bottom took up two walls. He began to open and close the cabinet doors, rifling through the contents.

"It's not a large or cumbersome painting. She could've stored it for later use."

Raven joined in the search without a word.

All of a sudden there was a commotion at the door, and he could hear a female and male talking.

"In here," he said, rushing to the utility closet door.

Raven hurriedly closed the cabinets and lunged inside just as the door swung open.

The closet smelled of paper and disuse. A thin strip of light slipped in at the base of the metal door. The rest of the cramped space was dark.

"That's strange. I thought I turned the light off."

The other occupant answered the professor from farther away, his words muffled. The desk chair rolled and creaked. Drawers slid open. Were they settling in for a long discussion?

Aiden shifted, his arm bumping hers, and she became keenly aware of his heat and bulk. They stood facing each other, almost touching. There wasn't room to move. Wasn't safe to move either, because they could knock something off the shelves marching up each wall.

Closing her eyes, she breathed in his woodsy scent and relived the kiss that had wiped her mind clean like a swipe over a dry-erase board. It had been reckless and unwise—and she wanted to repeat it.

She bowed her head, the brim of her hat catching on his shoulder. Her forehead unexpectedly found a place to rest on his firm chest. His hands closed over both of hers in warning. A ragged breath shuddered through him, and she forced her head up. His fingers slid away, and she sank her teeth into her lower lip.

The minutes stretched into an eternity. When she thought she might suffocate, the pair finished their meeting and left the room.

Aiden pushed open the door and sucked in air, as if he too had found their hiding place stifling. He reached over and adjusted her hat, his liquid brown eyes burning into her. Had he been fighting the same yearnings as her?

Raven dismissed the notion. He hadn't been pleased in the slightest about her lapse in judgment yesterday. He hadn't spoken more than necessary the rest of the night. Breakfast this morning had been awkward.

"Let's go through the rest," he said. "Then get out of here."

She retrained her focus on the task. As she'd suspected, they came up empty. The desolation in his expression gutted her. They didn't yet have evidence to warrant an arrest for the shooting incidents. Nor did they have anything to back up Aiden's claims.

"The maintenance area is in the basement. There's an office where odds and ends are collected, a sort of lost and found. Maybe it got put there."

She didn't have the heart to dissuade him. "Lead the way."

Aiden led her to the fire escape stairs instead of the central set they'd used before. They descended without passing another person. On the bottom level, he pushed open the bright blue door and met resistance.

A tall, slender gentleman grunted and stepped out of the way. She cataloged his shoes, dress pants, shirt and tie.

Aiden didn't look up. "Excuse us."

The man's breath hissed out in disbelief. Raven lifted her head and instantly recognized him. Desmond Whitlock. She snatched Aiden's hand. He looked up. Shock spread over his features.

"Coming back here is the last mistake you'll make." Hatred burning in his eyes, Desmond reached beneath his suit coat. Aiden called out a warning, and together, they ran deeper into the belly of the building. The openness of the public floors was not the layout down here. They traversed a network of hallways, the concrete walls an impenetrable maze.

Their sneakers squeaked on the polished tile floors. His dress shoes made a distinctive clicking noise that made it easy to track his pursuit.

They turned into a tighter, more dimly lit hallway. "I don't like this."

"Up ahead." He pointed to a single gray door with the exit sign above.

They burst out into the brisk night. This exit emptied into a vacant courtyard between the building and staff parking. If they could get to a protected spot, she could call in reinforcements. He grazed her arm and pointed to a round stucco building. "There."

They wove through the tables and leaped over the low stone wall, clabbering onto the swell of earth behind to reach the sidewalk above. The wound on her arm began to throb.

The sign on the round building advertised it as a student theater. Would it be open? Were there students inside who'd be at risk? As they neared the entrance, a bear of a man emerged from the hedges. A black hat and neck gaiter obscured his features, but she glimpsed a strip of white skin. Had to be Leonard. He held a gun fit with a silencer.

She stopped short, spun and put her hands on Aiden's chest. "Gun!"

He slung his arm around her and dragged her into the bushes. They came out on the other side and ran at full speed, ducking around trees and parked vehicles, avoiding lit areas where innocent bystanders might be. Leonard pursued them relentlessly but Desmond was nowhere in sight. Had he returned to his office, not wanting to risk being seen? Or had he perhaps gotten into his car to try to chase them down?

"We have to reach the sports complex," Aiden urged.

As they sprinted between tennis courts, her stomach tightened into a hard mass. She and Aiden had obeyed campus policy barring concealed weapons and left theirs in the glove box. Leonard and Desmond didn't feel the same compunction to follow the rules, and that put them in a vulnerable position.

She followed him to a yellow brick building. The first door was locked. The second one, too.

"Here." Aiden ushered her around the building to yet another door, which yielded to his touch. The racquetball courts were unoccupied. They entered a large, aged gymnasium with a volleyball court. He pointed to the wooden stands, and they ducked beneath them, crawling to the far corner of the narrow space. The air was heavy with the smells of wood varnish, popcorn and dirty socks.

Raven muted her phone and fired off a series of texts to Cruz and Silver, who promised to contact campus police. A door slammed. Heavy footsteps trod on the gym floor.

Aiden rested his hand on her shoulder. He'd placed himself between her and the opening, his determination to protect her at all costs unwavering.

TWELVE

Aiden's throat felt full of nails. His breathing was fast and loud, thanks to the sprint across campus. He used to run for fun and had built up his endurance, but his year of exile hadn't included time for exercise.

As Leonard's footsteps grew nearer to their hiding place, Aiden slowly shifted to face the opening, ready to give his life to spare Raven's. He prepared his speech. Somehow, he'd have to convince Leonard to take him and leave her. He would go with him willingly. He could even lie and say he had another flash drive hidden off campus to lure him away.

The man's construction-type boots entered his vision. Aiden started to move forward. Behind him, Raven snagged the sleeves of his hoodie.

"Don't." Her mouth was pressed against his ear, and the whisper was furious.

The door clanged again. "Hello? Sir?" A male voice carried through the gymnasium, accompanied by the jingling of keys. "We're getting ready to close up for the night. I was on my way to lock that last door when I saw you."

Raven's fingers twisted in the fabric, drawing it tight over his skin. Leonard must've lowered the neck gaiter. The man obviously hadn't seen Leonard's gun, or he wouldn't be approaching him.

There was a shuffling movement. "I apologize. I didn't realize the time."

Leonard's tone was mild. Casual. Masking his murderous intentions.

"I have to beat it over to the office. If I clock out late, my supervisor has a fit."

The speaker sounded like a young teenager, probably a first- or second-year student working a part-time job. *Please, God, protect us all.*

There was a long moment of silence. "I understand. I'll get out of your way."

"Sorry to inconvenience you. I have to follow the schedule, you know?"

Leonard followed him out of the gymnasium. They scrambled up from behind the stands.

"Campus police can scoop him up, right?"

Raven's expression was troubled. "He had a gun, but he didn't shoot at us."

"It's against campus policy to carry, though."

"He'd get a slap on the wrist, but it would preoccupy him long enough for us to return to Serenity."

She contacted the campus police department and identified herself. They ordered her to stay put. Within minutes, two officers, Kent and Nguyen, entered the gymnasium and listened to their account. They left out the part about the cheating ring and Aiden's return to the living. The less questions invited, the better. When Officers Kent and Nguyen gotten their information, they escorted Raven and Aiden to her car and promised to look for Leonard.

"He'll probably stash the gun and deny our version of what happened," Aiden said after they'd gone, tossing his hat and hoodie in the back seat.

"If they even find him tonight. But at least he'll be too busy avoiding them to hunt for us." As they entered the highway, she glanced at him. "Listen, Aiden, I know what you had in mind back there. You have to stop putting my safety above your own. I'm the law enforcement officer. It's my job to protect you."

She was asking the impossible. "We'll have to agree to protect each other."

"I've got your back, you've got mine?"

"Exactly."

His heart rate didn't settle into a natural rhythm until they reached Serenity's city limits. The close call was a reminder to be grateful for God's protection. The longer he'd spent hidden away in Louisiana, the more he'd focused on his problems. They'd grown to such proportions that he'd allowed them to eclipse God. The truth was He'd never forsaken him. He'd rescued him that night in the river. He'd provided for his basic needs. He was protecting him still.

Please help me to keep my focus on You, Lord.

Silver called and invited them to his house. Cruz was on his way over with dinner, and they could share updates about the case. Aiden gave Raven a thumbs-up sign, and she accepted the invitation.

When she ended the call, she looked over at him. "You're going to like his house."

"I'm intrigued."

She kept a vigilant watch on the rearview mirror. "It's private and secure, and he has a good alarm system. I haven't noticed anyone following us."

When she turned into the secluded cove, Aiden's gaze soaked in the three-story glass and timber structure built into the side of the mountain. He scooted forward.

"Think he'll give me a tour?"

Her laugh was sweet and husky.

The driveway climbed gently to the entrance on the top level. Silver opened the door before they had a chance to ring the bell and beckoned them inside. Aiden got lost in the details and missed the conversation. Raven nudged him in the ribs, her eyes alight with humor.

"Show him around first, please, Silver. Answer his questions. Otherwise, he won't pay attention to a thing we say."

Silver smiled and, leading him to the living area, launched into an explanation of the house and renovations he'd had done. The bedrooms were on the middle level. A home gym, indoor pool and office space occupied the bottom level. He mentioned Lindsey often, and it was clear he was eagerly anticipating their future together. Aiden felt that ugly emotion, jealousy, poking at him, and he confessed it in prayer immediately. He couldn't wallow in his own disappointments anymore. He had to rejoice with others and be grateful for what he did have.

They joined Raven and Cruz in the dining room, where they'd laid out their burgers, fries and onion rings from the Black Bear Café. The conversation inevitably shifted to their current problem, and Raven relayed their dismal lack of results.

Silver popped an onion ring in his mouth. Cruz sipped on his soda.

"I knew it wouldn't be a piece of cake," Raven

said, seated across from him. "But I thought we'd get at least one person to help us."

"We didn't make progress, either." Silver wiped his mouth with a paper napkin and wadded it up. "Jay's landlord is in failing health and has been in and out of the hospital. We weren't able to speak with him. The neighbors on either side of the rental moved in after Jay's death. The ones across the street remember him, but they don't recall anything significant about that night."

Cruz grunted. "A lot of time has passed."

"There were several houses behind Jay's," Aiden said. "Did you talk to any of those people?"

"One was vacant," Cruz supplied, dipping a fry in ranch dressing. "There was no one home at the other."

Raven folded her empty burger wrapper and stuck it into the sack. "You two should reach out to Jay's friends. Maybe one of them remembers Leonard visiting the house. Or maybe Jay confided in them, like he did with Aiden. In the meantime, I'm going ahead with my plan."

Silver and Cruz exchanged glances. "What plan?"

Her smile was self-mocking. "I'm going to pose as a college student."

Raven wasn't able to get a campus tour until Monday, and there were certain wedding preparations that couldn't be postponed. She stepped out of the dressing room Friday afternoon and into the bridal shop's luxurious sitting area. Sumptuous brocade sofas were situated around the central mirrors, providing Lindsey, her maid of honor, Thea, and the other bridesmaids a place to lounge. Aiden leaned against the far wall near a grouping of mannequins, arms folded over his chest and his expression indicating he'd rather teach design concepts to a rowdy kindergarten class than be involved in wedding fittings.

He'd ducked into a discount store that morning for warmer clothes. He'd purchased a blue, red and white flannel shirt, as well as a dark blue "I Love Tennessee" sweatshirt. Afterward, he'd noticed a barbershop next door and gotten a quick haircut. Her middle did a wild dance every time she looked at him. His shorn locks were shiny, with soft curls on top that enhanced his features.

At her entrance, his arms dropped to his sides. She read the appreciation in his wide eyes. When they were dating, he'd been liberal with compliments, leaving her in no doubt of his admiration.

"Fits you like a glove."

Lindsey's comment drew Raven's attention to the bride-to-be. Her smile hadn't wavered since they'd entered the shop. Although their case was far from resolved, Raven couldn't skip this important task or let her friend down.

Lindsey aimed a sly wink at Aiden over her shoulder. "What do you think, Aiden? Do you approve?"

The rest of the women's heads swiveled toward him. Red splashed across his cheekbones and he cleared his throat.

"I give it an A-plus."

At the behest of the shop employee, she stepped onto the dais and regarded her reflection. The deep rose, sleeveless dress had a fitted, shimmery bodice. It tucked in at the waist and then fell in floaty waves to the floor. The bandage on her arm was conspicuous, and she hoped the wound would heal before next weekend.

"It's perfect," Lindsey declared. "Aiden, should she wear her hair up or down?"

Raven shot her friend a *what are you doing* stare. Lindsey's teeth flashed behind her red-lipped smile.

He held his palms up. "I'm not an expert on women's hairstyles."

"Surely you have an opinion," Lindsey prompted.

"With that dress, definitely up." He gestured to the other section of the shop that housed the dresses and made a noise in his throat.

When he'd gone, Raven arched a challenging brow. "You're incorrigible."

"I simply want you to be as happy as I am."

"Happiness isn't on my radar." She was too busy trying to stay alive.

Her friend's smile faded, and she grasped Raven's hands. "I can't forget how sad you were, believing he was gone forever. You have a second chance with the love of your life. Don't waste it."

There was a commotion in the other room, and she heard Mason's deep voice greeting Aiden. Tessa strode into the viewing area with her young daughter, Lily. They were bundled in coats, gloves and scarves. The temperature had plunged overnight, and the clouds threatened snow. No doubt a shock for them, returning to this after a week in the sun and sand.

"Tessa, you made it." Lindsey hurried over. "How was your vacation?"

"We couldn't have asked for more perfect weather. Lily wanted to stay on the beach from dawn until dusk."

The little girl clutched her sparkly stuffed horse to her chest. "When can we go back, Mommy?"

Tessa laughed, her black curls quivering. "I'm not sure, ladybug. I'll have to talk to your dad."

Lindsey squatted before Lily and engaged her in conversation. Tessa crossed the room, saying a brief hello to the other ladies.

She hugged Raven, and the cold from her coat made Raven shiver. "Mason told me everything.

I can hardly believe it…your fiancé back from the dead."

"The shock hasn't completely worn off," she admitted. Some mornings when she first woke, she wondered if she'd dreamed Aiden's return.

"Mason was really worried about you all."

"Maybe we shouldn't have told him." This had been their first family vacation since reuniting last spring, and they deserved to enjoy their time away.

Tessa laid her hand on Raven's arm. "He would've been upset if you hadn't. You're part of his family. Our family."

When Tessa had first arrived in Serenity with a surprise daughter in tow, Raven hadn't welcomed her with open arms. She'd been outraged on Mason's behalf. Her attitude had softened as she learned the extenuating circumstances and got to know Tessa. She considered her one of her closest friends now.

"I've been praying for you," Tessa said. "I know there's not much I can do, but I'd like to at least supply meals. You certainly don't have time to shop or cook. Mason's mother and I will have a cooking day tomorrow."

"That's kind of you, Tess."

Mason entered the room, his intense brown gaze searching for her. When he strode over and enveloped her in a bear hug, a shaft of emotion took her by surprise. Mason wasn't just her superior. He was like a brother.

He eased out of the embrace and cupped her shoulders. "Whatever you need, I'm here for you."

He hadn't shaved while on vacation, and his dark hair was rumpled from the long drive.

Unable to speak around the lump in her throat, she nodded. *Have I thanked You, Lord, for my friends?*

"Tomorrow, after the bridal luncheon, we're going to meet at the stables and discuss the case," he said. "I want to know everything."

The shop employee intervened, inviting Tessa to try on her dress. Raven changed back into her jeans and sweater, looped her jacket over her arm and returned to the sitting area. She told Lindsey, Tessa and the others goodbye. Mason was in the other room talking to Aiden, and Lily was dancing around their legs, her stuffed pony held high. After being strapped in her car seat for hours, she was brimming with energy.

When she saw Raven, she altered course. "Where's Thorn? When can I see him?"

Raven smiled down at her. "He's at the stables right now, probably eating his supper." Cruz and Silver had offered to cover for her so she could leave work early. "He'd love a visit from you.

When the weather warms up, your dad will let you come ride again."

"When will it warm up?"

She glanced out the windows at the gray, blustery day and grimaced. "Your guess is as good as mine, kiddo."

Lily ran over to her dad and leaned into his legs. He boosted her into his arms and kissed her cheek. He'd adapted to fatherhood with ease.

Aiden's expression was inscrutable as he observed the pair. Was he thinking about their conversations about their future? They'd both expressed a desire for lots of kids.

"Do you have a horse, too?" Lily eyed Aiden.

The serious lines of his face softened, and he smiled. "No, I don't. I'd like to someday, though. Do you know how to ride? Raven taught me."

"My daddy showed me how." Her arms tightened around Mason's neck. "He won't let me fall."

Mason chuckled. "You've got that right, ladybug."

She cocked her head. "Are you a peace officer?"

For a moment, Aiden looked confused. Raven touched his arm. "Police officer."

"No, I'm a teacher."

Her face brightened. "Mommy says I'm going to start kindergarten this year."

"That will be fun." Aiden reached out and touched the pony. "Maybe you can take your friend with you to school."

"Oh, I can't do that."

Mason's brows lowered. "Why not?"

"I have to leave him with Mommy so she's not lonely."

The adults shared a smile. Raven's stomach grumbled, and Aiden arched a brow at her. "Time for supper?"

"Past time."

"Want us to follow you home?" Mason asked.

"No, thanks. I texted Cruz a few minutes ago, and he's going to meet us there as soon as he's finished at the stables."

"Keep your eyes and ears open."

"Will do."

Outside, a steady, bone-penetrating rain had her yearning for a toasty fire in the hearth, a thick blanket and steamed milk. They hurried to her car, blasted the heater and flipped on the windshield wipers.

"Happy that's over?" She buckled in.

He shrugged. "I wish you could linger with your friends and not have to worry about another attack."

"We'll get to do that tomorrow at the bridal lunch. Lindsey reserved a popular bed-and-breakfast with a restaurant. Mason and the guys will stand guard."

"I met Tessa briefly. She was friendly. Mason's little girl is cute."

"Lily has an endless supply of energy. She's a sweet thing, though. Tessa is a wonderful woman. Kind and generous. Compassionate. Somehow she wasn't tainted by her less-than-desirable upbringing in a Mafia family."

"Mason's a blessed man," he said quietly. "I'd give anything to have a family of my own."

Her throat full of acrid disappointment, she backed out of the parking lot and merged onto the main road. The shop was located between Serenity and Pigeon Forge, and they had miles of curves to navigate.

"You'll get your life sorted," she croaked out.

"Do you ever think about the plans we made for our own wedding?"

Her fingers dug into the wheel. "Sometimes."

She'd purchased magazines and scoured websites for ideas. She'd even tried on a couple of wedding dresses. Thank goodness she hadn't purchased one or put a deposit on a venue.

"You?"

He nodded. "I had too much time to think."

"The isolation must've been torture. You had a passion for teaching and thrived in the academic environment."

"I missed interacting with the students. Challenging them. Seeing them grow in confidence. I missed church services, too. Worshipping with other believers."

"You didn't go to church in Louisiana?"

"I didn't want to make friends and possibly put them in harm's way. I didn't know if Leonard and his cohort had ways of tracking me down." He stared out the passenger window. "I watched sermons on the TV in my room. There was also a Gideon Bible."

"You didn't have a laptop?"

"I left Tennessee with the clothes on my back."

"How can you not be bitter about everything you lost? The hardships you endured?"

"I've had my bouts of self-pity and anger, trust me. Ultimately, I have no one to blame but myself. I chose to play amateur sleuth. I chose to confront them. Jay's dead because of those choices, and now your life is in jeopardy."

Raven didn't have a chance to respond. "We have company."

THIRTEEN

Aiden twisted in the seat and saw a green Bronco bearing down on them. Daylight was fading fast, and the rain blurred everything, but there was no mistaking that vehicle. Dread slithered over his skin.

"That's Leonard's vehicle. How did he find us?"

Raven blew out a breath. "Desmond didn't pursue us across campus. He could've doubled back and placed a tracker on my car in case Leonard didn't finish us."

Leonard's boldness troubled him. Two dead bodies on campus would've generated a media storm and intense police scrutiny. He was getting desperate.

The Bronco knocked into their rear end, and Raven fought to keep the car steady. The two-lane road wound through dense woods. There were no businesses or homes around that he could see.

Aiden grabbed her phone from the console. "I'm calling Silver."

Before he could complete the call, Leonard rammed them again. This time, the tires lost their grip on the slippery asphalt, and they skidded off the road. A large tree loomed as Raven jerked the wheel. The rear left panel slammed into the tree, and the force jarred his entire body.

They both lurched forward and would've gone through the windshield if not for their seat belts. Her phone flew out of his hand, bounced off the dash and crashed to the floor.

"Raven?"

She blinked. "I'm not hurt. You?"

"No." The Bronco idled nearby. From this angle, he could see a second man in the cab. The passenger side door opened. "We have to go."

Raven removed their weapons from the glove box.

"Take my phone," she said, putting her weight into opening her door. He slid his into his pocket and, after unbuckling, climbed out on her side. They stayed low, using the car as a shield. Bullets started to fly. Windows popped.

He and Raven returned fire while trying to conserve ammo.

"Time to run," she said grimly. "You go first. Zigzag patterns. Use trees for cover."

He did as she instructed, running as fast as

he could up and over the slight incline. The rain made running on the layers of dead leaves treacherous. The terrain unfolded in a series of wooded, rolling hills. Shadows grew thicker the farther they got from the road.

Leonard and his cohort pursued them, still taking shots. Some of the bullets were so close they stirred the air near his face.

Raven was right behind him, and he didn't even know if he was leading her in the right direction. He tripped and went down hard on his left knee. Raven skidded down beside him, breaths coming in short bursts. He could barely make out her features.

"We have to find a place to hunker down," she said, winded.

She was right. Running in the dark—in the cold rain, no less—could earn them broken limbs.

"Hear that?" she whispered.

He listened for the men's advance. Instead, his ears detected a slight pinging noise. "Ice."

The raindrops that had made the chase precarious had turned to ice, and it felt like tiny blades on his exposed skin.

"You think they're still out there?" His vision couldn't penetrate the spaces between the trees.

"Not sure. I doubt they'd leave their vehicle on the road for long. A passing motorist would stop and summon authorities after seeing my wrecked car."

"That's a good thing. Let's circle back."

"I'm not familiar with this area, and I'm not sure I could get us back to the road. We have limited visibility. Temperature is dropping." She wiped her face with her sleeve. "Did you get my phone?"

He fished it from his pocket and handed it over. She pressed the buttons, and the cracked display lit up, briefly illuminating her features. "No service." She huffed her impatience. "At least we can use the flashlight feature."

The report of a gunshot sounded loud in his ears. Raven dived to the ground, landing on top of him. He shifted and, curving his arm around her waist, rolled them behind the nearest tree. Another shot landed in the trunk, spitting out a shower of bark.

They hustled as fast as they dared over the next ridge and then the next. How many miles they traveled, Aiden had no idea. His muscles ached. Thanks to the glacial onslaught, his jaw was stiff and his hair dripping wet. His sneakers were blocks of ice, making his footing less sure.

"Aiden." Her fingers grazed his. "Look."

Through the gloom, he saw a halo of white. They followed the source, which turned out to be an electric pole lamp. The dim globe illuminated a white structure with a gabled roof and arched stained glass windows.

"Church?"

She pointed to the aged, broken sign. "Wedding chapel."

She strode ahead, then jostled the doorknob. Locked. He followed her around to the back, his senses on high alert. While they were bathed in light, the woods were shrouded in darkness. That gave their enemies the advantage. Aiden didn't think he'd ever get used to being hunted like a prized buck.

"This one's locked, too." Standing beneath the overhang, she held out her hand. "Do you have any sort of card in your wallet? Store loyalty? Library?"

He handed her his useless debit card and watched her deftly work it to unlock the door. "Not sure if I should be impressed or not."

"It's one of the first things they teach you at the academy," she joked, striving for a lighthearted tone.

The interior had the distinct odors of disuse—damp wood and dust-coated seat cushions. He was able to make out pews bisected by a narrow aisle and a podium in the front. Although the windows appeared intact, the temperature inside was no better than outside.

Raven wiped her finger on the pew and grimaced at the coating of dust. "This place either has the worst cleaning crew in Tennessee or it's been out of business for a while."

He walked the length of the aisle. Between Silver and Lindsey's upcoming nuptials and hiding out in a wedding chapel, of all places, he couldn't escape the constant reminders of his and Raven's broken dreams.

"What are you thinking?"

He placed his hand flat on the podium. "That if I had overlooked the cheating, Jay would be alive. No one would be in danger. You and I might've gotten married, after all."

She grasped his jacket sleeve and pulled him gently around. "You did the right thing, Aiden. That's not always easy or convenient. While I disagree with your decision to play dead, our relationship problems aren't related." Her shoulders slumped. "The night of the party, I overheard your mom and her friends. She was very unhappy about your choice of bride. She didn't approve of my career. Thought you should've chosen someone more suitable, someone in the education field."

Aiden cringed inside. He could picture the ugly scene based solely on the hurt and disillusion in Raven's voice. "I had no idea."

"The worst part? She was worried that our kids would inherit my dyslexia."

Aiden fought a wave of anger. Reining it in, he cupped her upper arms. "I'm sorry you had to listen to that. It's unacceptable. You were a guest in her home. To publicly humiliate you…" He clenched and unclenched his teeth. "My mother has many fine qualities, but she has a critical view of the world. She also has impossible standards when it comes to her only son. I'll speak with her. She owes you an apology, at the very least."

"Your mom's words confirmed my own misgivings about our incompatibility. My learning struggles created insecurities that are part of my makeup. Those experiences marked me. I had reservations about going out with a professor—a doctor in his field, at that. I ignored them. I didn't let myself think long term."

Stung, he let his arms fall to his sides. "Do you regret what we shared?"

She gave a small shake of her head. "You made my world bigger, brighter, better. You became my best friend, Aiden."

His heart spasmed. How could that be true when she hadn't trusted him? Had given up so easily on them?

Pushing down his hurt, he tried to keep his voice controlled. "I wish you'd gotten the help you deserved in the beginning. That you didn't have to be alone in your struggle." He didn't kid himself into thinking the education system was perfect. Some students fell through the cracks. Sadly, Raven had been one of them.

Her skewed self-perception didn't have to be an insurmountable obstacle between them. Getting her to see that, however, might not be possible. Why even try?

A thud sounded on the front door. Then another. The frame quivered with tension.

He grabbed her hand and raced for the exit.

Raven and Aiden stumbled through the slick, jagged terrain. The noises behind them seemed to be from one person. The men must've decided to split up, one retrieving the Bronco while the other continued the hunt. She'd wrongly assumed that she and Aiden would ride out the night in the chapel—cold but protected from the elements. Ice crunched beneath her shoes. Her wet hair molded to her skull and neck, chilling her to the bone. She not only had to worry about bullets, but hypothermia, as well.

She lost her footing, grasping at a tree branch to keep from falling. The brittle wood snapped, and her hip thumped against the ground, sending a jolt of white pain through her leg. Aiden was beside her in a flash. He hefted her up, curled his arm around her waist and assisted her over the hill's crest. Although he didn't speak, determination emanated from him. He didn't falter. Didn't complain.

"Hey, Ferrer, you're never going to win, you know!"

The bellowed taunt halted Aiden in his tracks. His arm fell away, and he angled toward the direction of the voice.

She seized his hand and tugged. Hard.

He didn't budge.

"I'll track you down." The voice she assumed belonged to Leonard had an almost gleeful excitement to it. "I'm an expert at wounding my prey and waiting as they battle death. They always lose, and you will, too."

The words painted a grisly mental image. Raven pressed her fingertips into his inner wrist, communicating the need to keep going. After a few tense moments, he heeded the signal and threaded his fingers through hers. They picked their way through the undulating hills, skidding down the steeper slopes. Their progress was painstaking and loud.

Raven's free hand repeatedly drifted to her weapon tucked in its holster. She had decided to preserve her ammo and not shoot randomly into the darkness. With an expert hunter like Leonard, there was no telling the assortment of weaponry he had at his disposal. If they could find a makeshift shelter, they could fend him off.

And they needed one sooner rather than later. Ice coated everything in their path, and it showed no signs of stopping. Neither she nor Aiden were dressed appropriately for inclement weather. No gloves. No hats. Unlined jackets that provided minimal warmth.

The simple act of putting one foot in front of the other was becoming difficult. She had no sense of direction. Exhaustion made her almost dizzy, and she longed for an uninterrupted night of sleep in her toasty bed.

Leonard shot another round, and they both dropped onto their bellies. His laughter rang out, echoing through the night. His carelessness indicated he had plenty of ammo to spare, and that worried her.

She lay there for a minute, her cheek pressed against the wet, musty earth and considered staying put. Her energy stores had been depleted. Maybe just a short nap...

"Raven." Aiden's lips skimmed her ear, his breath blessedly hot. "We can't stop."

"I'm tired."

"I know." His tone was grim, bordering on angry. "Sleep will come later."

He hooked his hand beneath her arm and gave a giant heave. She somehow found the strength to get onto her knees and push her way to her feet. When she swayed, he was there to support her weight, his hands framing her waist. She couldn't resist resting her head against his chest.

"Mmm." He was solid and strong and smelled like happy times.

Aiden shifted away and framed her face with his hands. She grimaced at the cold touch.

"It's too dangerous for me to try to carry you," he whispered furiously. "I need your help, sweetheart. I need you to walk on your own steam. We have to find a place to get warm and dry."

Her muddled thoughts zeroed in on one word. "You called me *sweetheart*."

"Ready to give up, Ferrer?" a distant voice called. "What about your girlfriend, Officer Hart?"

She closed her eyes and remembered being Aiden's favorite person.

Aiden exhaled in a furious huff. "Maybe this will snap you out of it," he muttered.

His mouth came down on hers, insistent and demanding. Stars burst behind her eyelids. Unlike his Popsicle fingers, his kiss was as hot as a campfire. His touch sizzled and popped through her, calling forth sweet, sweet memories of kisses past.

When he started to step away, she seized his jacket lapels and held him fast. This was happiness. Aiden loving her.

He grasped her shoulders and lifted his head. "Awake now?" He sounded breathless and unsure.

Awareness of their situation—and the reason for his kiss—jolted her out of her stupor.

"I'm awake," she mumbled. Brushing past him, her legs like jelly, she forged ahead. Embarrassment burned off the cold-induced mental numbness.

Aiden followed in her wake without speaking. Smart man.

They walked for hours more. Or maybe it was minutes. She couldn't be sure at this point. Every step was precarious.

"There." Aiden snagged her sleeve.

To their right was a structure no bigger than an outhouse. The door was only wide enough for one person to enter at a time. Once inside, she fumbled with the phone. Her trembling fingers had trouble activating the buttons, but she managed to turn on the flashlight.

"There's nothing in here."

"Smells faintly of tobacco," he said, closing the door. "We've got to be near the national park border. Maybe this is part of an old homestead. If we keep going, we may find a cabin or barn."

"Or not," she retorted, still stung. "You can scout for a more comfortable location if you'd like, but I'm staying put."

She flicked off the light. Her back against the

wall, she slid down to the ground and pulled her knees to her chest.

Aiden sat close beside her. "That kiss wasn't my brightest idea, but you were starting to scare me."

His nearness taunted her. If she shifted a couple of inches to the right, she could curl into him and share his body heat.

"Cruz must be missing us by now," he said.

"I hope so. They would've initiated a search of the roads. As for pinpointing our current location, I don't know how long that will take."

Would they freeze to death before help arrived? Or get pinned in by Leonard?

Father God, we're in a desperate situation here. Please don't let our enemies win. Please give Aiden a chance to finish what he started and bring these perpetrators to justice. Give him a fresh start. Heal my heart. Heal us both.

Her poor heart couldn't take much more. Being with Aiden, the only man she'd ever loved, was killing her.

And then there was a commotion outside, and she moved into a crouched position, her weapon pointed at the door.

FOURTEEN

Aiden's weariness evaporated. He pushed his body back up the wall until he was on his feet again and pulled his gun from his holster. He could barely make out Raven's outline in the grimy darkness. Whoever was on the other side was going to be greeted by her Glock 19.

Men's voices leaked into their hiding space. He tensed.

Their interaction escalated to an argument, and they seemed to be moving closer. Was it Leonard and his friend? They never did identify the man who'd ambushed them inside his parents' house.

The chilly, damp air inside the shed seemed to contract. His head throbbed.

The sounds drifted off. Silence once again draped over them.

Raven's movements indicated she'd lowered her gun. "What just happened?"

"I thought for sure we were headed for a deadly confrontation."

"I can only guess at the reason we were spared. The important thing? God directed them elsewhere."

"For now."

She resumed her seat on the unwelcoming ground. "We've got to stay put until dawn."

Aiden sat beside her, trying not to think about the deep-dish pizza she'd promised and how long it had been since lunch. He tried not to dwell on his physical discomfort. Minutes passed in silence, and he started to get sleepy.

"This reminds me of the time we camped in Cades Cove." He fought the downward slide of his eyelids. They'd gone with another couple, the women sharing one tent and he and his friend sharing the other. "It was early April, and the temperatures dipped into the low forties. I could not get warm."

A husky laugh burst out of her. "I couldn't find my sleeping bag, so I brought my bed comforter. Big mistake. Although Angela didn't fare much better in her sleeping bag. The coyotes howled for hours. There was no sleeping that night."

He let his head fall back against the wall and crossed his arms over his chest. "I could go for some s'mores."

She groaned. "With peanut butter cups instead of milk chocolate squares."

"You don't mess with an original, Raven."

"If I recall, you refused to even try it."

"I didn't need to."

"You're missing out."

He closed his eyes, his mind going back to that camping trip. They'd gone on many more, mostly in and around the national park and with the same friends. Aiden relished being in nature. Having Raven at his side had made the experience all the sweeter.

"How cold are you?"

He opened his eyes and turned his head, wishing he could drink in her beauty. "Cold enough to risk your ire."

Looping his arm around her shoulders, he pulled her into his side. She came willingly, then tucked her head beneath his chin and slipped her hand under his jacket. He wrapped his other arm around her, completing the circle. He'd missed this. Simply holding her—whether they were stargazing beside a campfire, watching the river trickle past in her backyard or snuggling on his couch listening to music. Being comfortable together, enjoying each other's company without having to say a word had been a treasure.

He sighed and prayed for resolve. Kissing her would be so natural…and wrong on many levels.

Aiden didn't mean to, but he drifted off to sleep. A rumbling noise vibrated through the shed and jarred him awake. He couldn't be sure how much time had passed. The darkness wasn't as thick as before. Raven was a deadweight against him, like a marble carving.

Adrenaline poured through him. "Raven, wake up."

She didn't respond. He skimmed her cheek and found the pulse point on her throat. The steady throb reassured him. "Raven?"

The out-of-place noise passed overhead again, and he realized it was the thump of helicopter blades.

She moaned. Bracing her hand on his chest, she sat upright. "How long…" Her voice sounded raw.

"No idea. There's a helicopter out there. We have to try to get their attention."

The tourist helicopters wouldn't be operating at night. It could be an air ambulance on its way to an accident. Or it could be the sheriff's department. He stood up, opened the door and stumbled outside, waving his arms and yelling. Raven followed suit, using her phone light to attract attention.

The helicopter circled overhead. He experienced a flicker of doubt. Leonard's buddies surely didn't own one, did they?

As it landed somewhere north of them, he prayed he hadn't summoned their enemies. He grasped her hand tightly. Together, they picked their way through the sparse trees. The wintry storm had ceased pelting the earth with ice, but the remaining cold was excruciating, making even his teeth ache. The subfreezing temperature had kept the ice on the ground from melting.

The breeze kicked up by the slowing blades sliced through him. His hair and clothes were damp, his skin clammy.

As they entered the field, he noted the sheriff's department logo with relief. A tall, imposing figure emerged, and the lights glinted off his pale gray hair.

Silver jogged over to them, his face taut with worry. "We've been over this area twice before and were about to give up the search."

"We fell asleep," Aiden said.

His violet gaze raked over them and, seeing no obvious injuries, gestured behind him. "Let's get you warmed up."

Silver buckled Raven into her seat and covered her with a blanket. The fact she allowed the coddling was an indication of her extreme exhaustion. Aiden settled into the seat beside her and listened as Silver introduced them to the pilot. This was his first time in a helicopter, and he was too dazed and tired to enjoy it.

They put on their headsets, and the aircraft lifted off.

"Cruz got to your house and reported your absence. Then someone called in the accident. When the tags were linked to your name, Raven, an officer contacted Mason. We considered coming out on horseback to search, but Lieutenant Hatmaker forbade it. What happened exactly?"

Raven's explanation seemed dragged from somewhere deep inside her. Aiden found her hand beneath the blanket and linked their fingers. She turned her head without lifting it from the seat and gave him a ghost of a smile.

The pilot landed at the Serenity Police Station, where they were met by the police chief and an ambulance. When further medical treatment was deemed unnecessary, Silver drove them to Raven's. The sky had lightened to a soft gray, but they weren't ready for anything other than a quick snack and a few hours of uninterrupted sleep. Silver claimed the couch, leaving Aiden the room that used to belong to Lindsey. After he and Raven had taken hot showers, they collapsed into their respective beds. Aiden, at least, was out like a light within moments.

The bridal lunch was postponed until that evening in consideration of Raven's ordeal. When they'd woken in the early afternoon, Silver had informed her of the schedule change. Thankfully, the bed-and-breakfast had been willing to accommodate them. Aiden would've felt even worse than he already did if she'd missed the important event.

Lindsey had every right to complain, but she'd been more concerned about their welfare than her celebration.

"Sure you don't want to go inside where it's warm?" Mason's breath hung like a vapor. The restaurant lights spilled through the windows like beckoning amber flames. Silver, gold and red heart stickers adorned the panes in a nod to the coming holiday.

"I'm tempted," he admitted. "But the ladies don't need me to crash their party. Besides, Raven made sure I came prepared." He was wearing multiple layers, including a borrowed police jacket, beanie and gloves. The sun had appeared long enough that day to melt the ice, but it still wasn't pleasant to be outside, especially after sunset.

Mason scrubbed at his jaw. "I know one in particular who wouldn't mind."

Aiden glanced through the window, hoping for a glimpse of long, coal black hair and warm honey eyes.

"She took your absence hard, you know," he said, drawing Aiden's attention once more.

"She had more trouble than usual concentrating. Couldn't sleep. She refused to discuss her grief. The guys and I were really worried for a while. I have to ask—are you planning on pulling another disappearing act?"

"Since it didn't accomplish anything other than delaying the inevitable? No."

"Good to hear. You're better off working in conjunction with our unit." He shoved his hands deep in his jacket pockets. "Raven told me about her latest plan."

"Going undercover as a transfer student?"

"It's a solid idea. Maybe this is the way to get a student to testify to what's happening on campus."

Aiden didn't relish the thought of her being on campus alone. Raven couldn't go through the proper channels for permission to sit in on a class, and to gain the trust of a classmate would take time they didn't have. So she'd opted for a campus tour with a student orientation leader, figuring she could learn more during an informal interaction. Raven had gone to the university website and scheduled a tour for Monday morning, adding a request for a student athlete.

"She doesn't want me on campus." He kicked at a stray rock on the pavement. "It's difficult to do nothing while she puts her life on the line."

"Tessa isn't an officer, but I got a taste of what

that might feel like when her brother was dogging our heels, trying to kill her and kidnap Lily. It's where faith comes into the equation. Faith that God has everything under control and that He'll supply the grace and strength we need when trials come." He settled his hand on Aiden's shoulder. "The two of you have my prayers."

Mason's words startled him. He'd forgotten what it was like to have a friend, and one who was a believer, at that.

"Thanks, Mason."

He yearned for a glimpse of normal life. Would he ever make his way back to that? To a job, a home, a church? Friends? Hobbies? Would it mean as much without Raven by his side?

Silver and Cruz walked up. "I got a call from the neighboring county's sheriff's department. There was a tracking device on Raven's car."

Frustration boiled in his veins. "Why isn't Leonard being arrested? He ran us off the road. The crime scene investigator can verify that."

"It didn't happen in our jurisdiction," Cruz answered. "And the responding deputy hasn't been on the job long. He assumed it was a single vehicle accident. He had her car towed because it was blocking the narrow passage through that section."

Aiden clenched his fists. Raven had reached out to the university police officers who'd responded to their call after their run-in with Leonard. By the time they'd caught up with him, he'd disposed of the gun and vehemently denied being involved. He lied about his whereabouts, and Desmond corroborated his alibi.

"What about the bullet casings on the side of the road?"

Cruz ran his hand over his spiky black hair. "I have spoken to their sheriff's department. They're going to revisit the accident site tomorrow. They're also willing to bring him in for questioning but are having trouble locating him."

Mason's eyes narrowed. "He has to be feeling the heat. Aiden, is it possible for him to get time off in the middle of a semester?"

"He can claim an illness or death in the family. The university would arrange for a sub or a teaching assistant to take over."

Chatter and laughter preceded the women as they trickled out of the restaurant. His gaze zeroed in on the statuesque beauty sandwiched between her friends. Raven's red dress was visible beneath her black peacoat. The filmy fabric floated around her long legs and skimmed her calves. Black wedge shoes added a boost to her height, making her tower over petite Lindsey. Her hair formed a glossy black waterfall to the middle of her back.

A bright smile stretched her cheeks, and her

expression sparkled with good humor. His heart squeezed. Seeing her happy made him happy. He wanted it to last.

Lindsey was the first to break away from the group. She sashayed up to Silver and wrapped her arms around his neck. "I missed you."

His expression softened like butter, and his eyes ate her up. He settled his hands on either side of her waist. "I'm yours for the next hour or so, then I have to catch up on my beauty sleep." He winked.

Cruz rolled his eyes. "You've been apart what? Two hours?"

Mason chuckled as Tessa sidled into his side. "That's jealousy talking." He kissed her forehead.

Silver only had eyes for his fiancée. He didn't acknowledge anyone else's presence as he leaned in for a brief but tender kiss.

Aiden remembered what that was like. Raven stood slightly behind the other couples, and the lightheartedness he'd admired minutes ago had been replaced with sadness and regret. Reality had set in, reminding her that their lives had been irrevocably altered.

Her partners were acting as bodyguards during their off-duty hours, and no one knew if he or Raven would live until the ceremony.

FIFTEEN

Raven spent Sunday recovering from the week-end's events. She and Aiden prepared breakfast and ate on the couch while watching her church service online. They'd remained indoors the rest of the day while patrol officers took turns with guard duty. She'd caught up on laundry, and Aiden had made calls to his friend, Pete, and his parents. He hadn't mentioned her confession again. Or the kiss. She tried to put both out of her mind and focus on the campus tour.

As she approached the cafeteria, she caught a glimpse of her reflection. So far, everyone had appeared to accept she was a sophomore in college looking to transfer schools. She had her friend Lorie's daughter, seventeen-year-old Shania, to thank. Shania had instructed her to go for a fresh-faced look using minimal makeup and had lent her a popular brand sweatshirt and leggings. Raven had also left her hair loose beneath a worn baseball cap.

She'd been placed in a small group of prospective students led by two orientation leaders—sophomores Esme Greene and Alexandria Bolton. Esme was a business major and played for the women's basketball team. While friendly, she wasn't the chatty type. Alexandria, on the other hand, was much more sociable. Apparently, she was a top-notch volleyball player. There wasn't time to ask personal questions during the tour, so Raven suggested having lunch together. Esme had unexpectedly agreed to tag along.

"You're interested in playing volleyball?" Esme asked now, perusing the cafeteria options.

"For the university team, not just intramural sports," Raven answered. "Although, I've had trouble keeping my grades up at my current college. English is my worst subject. Even with tutoring, I barely passed. Athletes should get some leniency, you know?"

Esme pursed her lips. "You've got that right." Gesturing to the opposite line, she said, "I'm going for salad."

The three filled their plates and swiped their cards at the cash register. While searching for open seats, Raven's gaze snagged on a black-haired man whose back was to her. He was wearing a cap and hoodie with the university colors. Since he was hunkered over his tray, she couldn't get a good look at his face. But he shifted as she passed, giving her a glimpse of his profile, and she almost dumped her lunch on the polished tiles.

She shot him a glare over her shoulder. Aiden had disregarded her instructions to wait in the off-campus restaurant. He was in for a serious tongue-lashing.

Raven chose a seat facing the wide windows overlooking the street and tree-lined sidewalk. With him out of sight, she had a better chance of concentrating on her task instead of the scathing speech she'd like to give him. Leonard hadn't yet been located. Desmond was still a threat and their third suspect was an unknown player.

"What's your most challenging subject?" She twisted the cap of her flavored water.

Esme shrugged and picked up her fork. "I struggle with math and science. Words make more sense to me than numbers and formulas."

"This is your second year playing basketball, right? How do you and your teammates keep up with the demands of practice, travel time and games, not to mention schoolwork? I'll take any pointers I can get."

"Some girls are good at time management, I guess."

"They don't have a social life, you mean. No parties. No boyfriends."

She smiled in agreement. "Coursework isn't

a struggle for some. But that's not the case for everyone."

Alexandria, seated beside Esme, put down her phone and attacked her pizza. "I have trouble staying organized. I'm always working until the last minute to finish assignments. But I refuse to give up volleyball. I'll do anything to stay on the team, and I do mean anything. Esme feels the same."

Esme cast the other girl a quelling stare, but Alexandria merely shrugged. "What? It's true."

"I'm glad there's a way to check up on professors before we sign up for classes," Raven said into the stilted silence. "I'm going to try to find some lenient English professors. At my current school, there are ways to boost your grades. Money talks, if you know what I mean."

Esme's posture was stiff. Wary. "If you say so."

"Don't tell me that doesn't happen here. The athletics program is too important to this town."

Alexandria snorted. "If I knew who to bribe for better grades, I wouldn't be in the fix I'm in. I'd have more time on my hands for fun, that's for sure."

"Esme?"

Her lashes swept down as she speared a tomato. "I wouldn't know anything about that."

Raven changed the subject, keeping her tone

lighthearted. When they'd finished eating, Alexandria rushed off to a class on the far side of campus. Esme stood and slung her backpack over her shoulder. "I have to get to class. Do you know the way back to the visitors' parking?"

She did, of course, but she hadn't gotten the information she was seeking. "Can I walk with you?"

"Sure."

Raven sought out Aiden. His gaze probed hers. She arched an irate brow at him and followed Esme through the cafeteria and out onto the sidewalk. As they traversed the crosswalk, she scanned their surroundings for suspicious activity.

A couple of guys across the street yelled at Esme, and she waved in response. The one in the backwards hat asked when she was going to come over, and she just shook her head.

"They seem friendly," Raven said.

"There are lots of friendly guys on campus, but I have a boyfriend. His name is Kelvin. We met during freshman orientation and hit it off. Been together ever since."

"Does he play basketball?"

"Football."

"Is his name Kelvin Farley? The star quarterback?"

"That's right." Her shoulders straightened with pride. "There's a good chance he'll go pro."

Raven expressed the appropriate amount of awe. If anyone would feel pressure to keep up their GPA, it would be Kelvin. She didn't pose any more questions, however. She sensed she'd be shut out if she did.

At the visitor lot, she lifted her hand in a wave. "Thanks for your help today, Esme. I really appreciate it."

Her smile was genuine. "Nice meeting you, Jenny."

Raven waited until she got to her rental car to call Aiden. "Where are you?"

"Cafeteria."

"I'll pick you up."

Frustrated by Esme's reticence, she was ready to release some steam as soon as he got comfortable in the passenger seat. When he tugged off his cap and balanced it on his knee, however, much of the steam evaporated. She still wasn't used to his new look. The short style highlighted his bone structure and sculpted lips. Lips that had seared her out of near hypothermia.

"I was careful," he said.

"You took an unnecessary risk," she shot back. "Even if Desmond saw me, he likely wouldn't act in broad daylight and with students everywhere."

"Wasn't right for you to be alone," he said stubbornly.

"You forget that I'm the police officer, and you're the civilian. I call the shots in this case."

He sighed. "Trust me, that's something I won't forget. You think you have a problem with my profession? Imagine if I put myself in danger every time I walked out the door?"

"It's a good thing we're not a couple then, isn't it?"

His jaw clenched, and he stared straight ahead. Raven bit her lip.

The stress of the past week—and the uncertainty of what lay ahead—was getting to them.

She drove to a gas station adjacent to campus and close to several apartment buildings mixed in with older homes rented by students.

"Why are we here?" he asked.

"I'm certain Alexandria would've blabbed if she had any information." She killed the engine. "Esme, on the other hand, is not what I'd call an oversharer. She was reluctant to talk about the grade boosting, but I'm positive she knows something. She may even be involved. I'd like to speak to her again. This time, as Officer Raven Hart."

"She could turn on us."

"I don't have time to cultivate a relationship with this girl. Leonard is walking the cliff's edge, and he's about to leap off. Once that happens, he'll be relentless. He'll have nothing to lose. I'm confident I can get her to help us."

His somber brown eyes met hers. "I'm going with you." When she opened her mouth to respond, he held up his hand. "I'm not questioning your judgment. I simply want you to be extra cautious. You don't know what you might be walking into."

Raven wouldn't accept sitting idly by while he courted danger. So why should she expect him to?

"Fine. You be the lookout while I have a chat with Esme."

They spent hours in the rental car parked on the street near Esme's apartment. Silver had looked up her address for them. Esme rented one half of a duplex. Easy for them to surveil.

They took turns playing games on her phone. When they tired of that, she turned on her video playlist of eighties favorites and watched the occasional car cruise past. The neighborhood was quiet during the day while students were in classes. Foot traffic started increasing the later the hour grew.

She blew out another breath. "I could not do this on a regular basis."

Gathering her hair in her hands, she deftly braided the strands and secured the end with a band she wore around her wrist. The scent of her apple shampoo wafted over, teasing him. Her face was makeup-free, aside from a shimmery lip gloss. Aiden couldn't get enough of her. He'd been back in her life for just over a week, yet he already knew walking out of it again would be excruciating. Worse than the first time, in fact.

He dug into the plastic bag of snacks he'd gotten at the gas station. "What's your pleasure?"

Her eyes widened. Angling toward him, she surveyed the array of choices. Fruit-flavored candy squares, nougat and almond candy bar and peppermint chocolates. "You remembered my weaknesses."

He remembered everything about her.

"I don't know which one to choose." Her eyes sparkled with anticipation.

He chuckled. "What you don't eat now, you can save for later."

She snatched the candy bar, shucked the wrapper and took a bite. A blissful noise hummed in her throat. "Best candy bar ever."

He'd buy her a lifetime supply if it meant keeping that smile on her face.

A tan sedan rolled toward them and parked in the duplex driveway. Esme emerged, backpack dangling from her wrist, and headed for her front door.

Raven rewrapped the confection and placed it

in the glove box. Her badge tucked in her pocket, she pulled the door handle. "Ready?"

"Right behind you."

The chilly air was like a smack in the face. He huddled into his hoodie and hurried across the street, steps behind Raven. When Esme opened the door, surprise was chased by confusion across her face.

"Jenny?" Beneath her bangs, her brown eyes flicked to Aiden. "What's going on? How did you get my address?"

Raven slipped into official police business mode. "Esme, my name isn't Jenny, and I'm not a student. I'm Raven Hart, an officer with the Serenity Mounted Police."

Esme's eyes got big as Raven produced the badge. "Is he an officer, too?"

"No." Raven gestured past Esme. "We'll explain everything. Can we come in?"

"I don't know…"

"Esme, it's important we speak with you," Aiden said.

"About what?"

"The cheating ring," Raven supplied. "Leonard Grunberg."

Her jaw dropped. "You know about that?"

"Let's talk for a bit," Raven said firmly.

Esme responded to the authority in Raven's voice and allowed them to enter. The living room was small and cluttered with fashion magazines, nail polish bottles and jar candles. Raven helped herself to the sofa. Esme removed a stack of books from a plastic chair and perched on the edge, knees together, hands knotted. Aiden stationed himself by the windows with a clear view of both the living room and the street.

"Am I in trouble?" Her voice quivered.

Raven leveled a frank gaze at her. "Help us with this case, and I'll see that you get a deal."

"How did you find out?"

Aiden spoke up. "I uncovered the cheating ring last year. I'm Aiden Ferrer, by the way. I used to teach in the art and architecture department." There was no flicker of recognition. "I angered some people by trying to unearth the truth. I had to disappear for a while."

He didn't mention Jay's involvement. He didn't want to spook her in case she didn't already know what Leonard and the others were capable of.

Raven rested her hands on her knees and leaned forward. "Esme, this is serious. We need someone to help us."

Her expression became stormy. "You're expecting me to snitch."

"You want to stay out of jail?"

She sucked in a breath. "What about my scholarships? My basketball career?"

Aiden watched her grapple with the ramifications of her choices. Being expelled was a real possibility.

"I can't speak to those things because I'm not a school official."

Esme popped up and began to pace. "Maybe I should hire a lawyer."

Raven nodded, unruffled. "You have that right. However, if you choose that route, I won't be able to help you."

She tunneled her hands through her short, dark hair.

Raven sighed. "I know this is difficult, Esme. But you have the opportunity to get in front of this. If you won't help us, I'll offer the deal to someone else."

"What do you need exactly?" She had the air of a mouse cornered by a cat now.

"Evidence of the cash payments you made to Leonard. ATM receipts showing cash withdrawals. I'm assuming you didn't use checks."

She stopped chewing on a nail to shake her head.

"Any email correspondence between you and other students playing the system. Text messages. If you've deleted them, we can send your phone to our crime lab and retrieve the information."

Aiden turned at the hum of a car engine. "Someone's here."

He didn't recognize the muscular young man

emerging from the driver's side. Blond hair peeked from beneath his cap, and a bruise darkened his eye.

Esme gasped. "I forgot Kelvin's taking me to dinner."

Before Raven could respond, a key was inserted into the knob and the door swung inward. Kelvin halted on the threshold. Surprise rippled across his face, chased by recognition. He knew their faces. Why? How?

"Esme, what's going on?" he barked, not bothering to close the door. "Why are you talking to a cop?"

She rushed over and grabbed at his arm. "I swear I wasn't going to give them your name."

He jerked free, his gray eyes flinty. "But you were going to give them others? Do you have a death wish like Jay?"

Esme froze. "Jay drowned."

Kelvin jerked his hand to the door. "You're leaving. Now."

Aiden and Raven exchanged glances.

Esme gave his arm a shake. "Kelvin, what aren't you telling me?"

Aiden stepped forward. "Were you there when Jay was killed?"

His fists clenched, and his chin jutted. "Get lost, or I'm calling the landlord. You're trespassing."

Aiden's gut told him Kelvin had pertinent information. He opened his mouth to press for it, but Raven touched his arm and shook her head. She held out a business card to Esme. "The offer still stands. Call me."

Esme's gaze swept to the floor. Raven placed it on the coffee table.

They walked outside, and the door thundered closed behind them.

SIXTEEN

Aware of Kelvin watching from the window, Raven eased the car from the curb. "It's interesting that Kelvin threatened to call the landlord and not the police."

"He knows more than Esme."

"Let's double back around and find a spot farther down the street, out of their direct view. I'd like to see where Kelvin heads next." She considered Aiden's profile. "Unless you've had enough of waiting around."

He pulled out the snacks. "We've got sugar to sustain us."

"You're more of a salty guy, if I recall correctly."

He produced a second bag from beneath the seat, a grin softening the seriousness of his features. "Cheddar popcorn and honey mustard pretzels."

"We should pool our resources, Professor."

Their gazes locked. "Sweet and salty is a good combination," he said. "I'm in."

Smiling, she drove around the block and parked where they couldn't be seen from the apartment. "Let's check out Kelvin's social media, shall we?"

She scrolled popular sites for posts or photos that would give them insight into their case.

"Hold on." Aiden leaned into her space, attention fixed on the screen. "That's Jay."

In the picture, Kelvin and Jay were in their football uniforms on the playing field. They stood next to each other and were surrounded by other teammates. Jay had a bright smile, intelligent brown eyes and a boyish face.

"Kelvin didn't come up in our conversations," Aiden said. "Was Jay protecting him?"

"Maybe Jay didn't know he was involved. Or he didn't get into the cheating game until after Jay's death. I don't see anything helpful in these posts."

Aiden sank back in his seat while she continued to search. He immediately straightened. "Look."

Kelvin exited the apartment and, with a furtive glance around, got into his sports car and reversed out of the driveway. Raven waited a beat before entering the street. She hung back and prayed he wouldn't notice them. He drove away from campus and the downtown area, eventually turning down a street marked with more vacant lots than homes.

Kelvin pulled into a long gravel driveway. Raven slowed and eased the car to the street's edge a fair distance away, watching as Kelvin strode up to a gray clapboard house with black shutters, took the steep stairs two at a time and ducked beneath a faded metal awning. He was ushered inside by someone they couldn't see.

"This isn't Leonard's house." Raven texted Cruz the address and asked him to look into it. "Who are you here to see, Kelvin?" she murmured, almost to herself.

"Our visit to Esme rattled him."

"You saw his expression. He recognized us. Knew I was police."

"Kelvin fits the height and weight description of the man who accosted us inside my parents' house." Aiden's knee bounced incessantly. "Would Leonard enlist a college student's help, though?"

"That's what we're going to find out."

The next morning, Aiden helped the officers with the horses' morning routine. Raven had to go out on patrol with Cruz, while Mason and Silver paired off for another section of town. She couldn't continue to ditch her duties. They'd decided he would stay at the stables, outfitted with the latest security features, until their return.

When they were all in their uniforms, the horses saddled and ready, Raven didn't immediately follow the men outside.

"We'll work on the case this afternoon."

Leonard still hadn't been located. Desmond had put his head down and kept quiet. The house Kelvin had visited belonged to Arnold Decker, a transplant from Wyoming with no criminal history and no obvious links to any of the suspects. They'd hoped Zane or another student would relent and contact them. So far, none had.

"I'll spend the time getting my affairs in order. Coming back from the dead is turning out to be a painstaking process." The deep valley between her brows remained. "Stop fretting. I'll be fine. King and Iggy will keep me company."

Behind them, the two horses poked their heads out of the stalls. She smiled. "I think they're counting on you to keep them entertained."

"A hard job, but someone has to do it."

"I'll see you in a few hours."

"Be safe out there."

After the officers had gone, Aiden spent time with the horses before retreating to Raven's office. She'd given him permission to use her computer, and he spent the next hour on the phone with various officials, none of whom were too clear on what his next steps should be. When his patience had reached its limits, he resorted to scrolling through job listings. In Morganton, not Serenity. This town wasn't big enough for them both.

Around midmorning, he went in search of a snack. He changed course when an alert sounded from the small office tucked beside the front door. Cruz had given him a quick rundown on how to work the various systems. He recognized the woman at the gate.

Esme had obviously changed her mind about helping them.

He activated the speaker. "Hello, Esme."

She bit her lip. "Professor Ferrer? Is that you?"

"I'll unlock the gate. Park by the door."

Fingers clasping and unclasping the steering wheel, she nodded. He let her through and, after watching the gate close behind her car, went to let her in.

She hurried inside, head swinging left to right to look over her shoulders.

"Are you worried someone followed you?" he asked.

"I'm being paranoid." She ran manicured fingers through her short, streaked hair. "I wasn't sure if I should come. I called Officer Hart's cell multiple times, but it kept going to voice mail."

"She's on patrol." He extended his hand toward the break room. "We can talk in here."

Esme preceded him into the room. Vending machines lined the interior wall, and there was a kitchenette along the back, complete with coffee maker and supplies. Several tables offered plenty of space to spread out.

"Want something to drink? A snack?"

"I don't think so."

Ignoring the seat he pulled out for her, she wrung her hands. "Where is she?"

"Somewhere in Serenity. I don't know her exact location. You're welcome to stay here until she returns."

"When will that be?"

Aiden sat down, thinking she'd follow suit. She was wound tight. "Maybe an hour or so."

Esme blinked, licked her upper lip and dug into the purse slung across her body. When she produced a handgun and pointed it at him, Aiden's body flushed cold. Then a flash of ire surged through him. He was getting tired of people pointing guns at him.

He held his palms out and slowly stood. "What are you doing with that, Esme?"

There was a wildness in her eyes that made him uneasy. She was operating on pure emotion—she wouldn't be easy to reason with.

"I can't let you hurt Kelvin."

"I'm not going to hurt him." He inched away from the table. "Put the gun away. Let's discuss this."

"Stop moving!" she cried. Her hold on the gun was unsteady, and he froze, fearing she'd pull the trigger accidentally.

"Esme, does Kelvin know you're here?"

"No." She shook her head, her dangly earrings swaying. "No one does."

He inclined his head to the side. "The police will. You're on camera. If you go through with this, you'll spend the rest of your life behind bars."

She looked almost sick at that, but she didn't lower the gun.

"What are you protecting Kelvin from exactly?" He took another miniscule step closer. "He was there the night Jay was murdered, wasn't he? Kelvin helped Leonard."

"Kelvin didn't know what would go down that night. He's a pawn, don't you see? Leonard's poisoning his mind. Leonard's the one who deserves to go to jail, not Kelvin."

"Have you known all along?"

"He told me yesterday, after you left the apartment." She was visibly shaking, and her finger danced around the trigger.

"Easy, now." Sweat slid down his spine. "I understand why you're upset. You were friends with Jay, I gather?"

Tears shimmered in her brown eyes ringed with thick black liner. "He was truly kind, you know? Humble. Would do anything for anyone. He and Kelvin were tight. When I heard about his drowning, I was in shock. Jay rarely drank. I had questions. Doubts. Now I know the truth, and it hurts."

"Jay didn't deserve to die. Leonard and Kelvin have to pay for their crimes."

She scrubbed the wetness from her cheeks with her forearm. "Kelvin's innocent. He didn't strangle Jay. Leonard did."

"He didn't do anything to stop it, Esme." He spoke in a soothing tone. "That makes him an accessory to murder. I saw them together, moving Jay's limp body to the pool."

She jutted her chin. "Kelvin isn't thinking straight. I told you Leonard's the puppet master."

"Kelvin makes his own choices. You have a choice, too. Do the right thing, Esme. Put the gun away. Be on the right side. Help us."

"Help you? Not going to happen. He's too important to me."

Aiden thought he had more time, more words to bargain with. But Esme pulled the trigger, and the gun's blast rocked through him.

SEVENTEEN

The sound of a gun going off inside the stables sent terror ricocheting through Raven. She bolted for the side entrance, all thoughts of unloading the horses forgotten. Cruz's boots pounded close behind her.

Her fingers trembled on the alarm pad. *Please let Aiden be all right. Please.*

The silence was deafening. What could it mean? She'd recognized Esme's car and thought it meant she'd had a change of heart.

Raven skidded around the corner and would've flown straight into the break room had Cruz not been there. He seized her arm in warning. Her training and experience snapped into place, and she slowed, unsheathing her weapon and waiting for Cruz to get into position before assessing the situation.

Aiden was upright and coherent. There was no blood seeping from his person. In fact, he appeared to be in full possession of his faculties.

He stood, arms wide, blocking Esme from the 9mm pistol lying several feet away on the floor. Esme didn't appear to want it. In fact, she had recoiled in horror.

He jerked his head toward them, relief rippling across his features. "Good timing."

Raven entered with her weapon drawn. "We heard a gunshot."

"Esme fired at me, but it went wide."

Cruz retrieved an evidence bag and placed the 9mm inside. Raven walked over to the vending machine wall and inspected the bullet hole.

Esme didn't utter a word as Cruz read her her rights and cuffed her. When patrol officers arrived on scene, Cruz went to care for the horses. Aiden gave his statement, and Esme was taken into custody. When everyone had gone, Aiden thrust his hands through his short, wavy locks and sagged against the nearest table. "I let her in. Didn't think anything of it."

Raven put a hand on his shoulder. "Emotions can cloud reason and get people into trouble. Based on your statement, that's what I think happened to Esme. Kelvin told her how deep he's in with Leonard, and she panicked. Took matters into her own hands."

"What now?"

"If you're up to it, we confront Kelvin. Once

we explain what's happened to his girlfriend, maybe he'll flip on Leonard and Desmond."

"Why wouldn't I be up to it?" He looked sincerely bewildered.

She rested her palm on his chest. "You narrowly missed a bullet. Again. Things like that wear on a person. It's tough even for seasoned officers."

"I can't dwell on it. I have to keep moving forward."

Raven had never considered Aiden less capable than the men she worked with. She hadn't questioned his courage or wondered how he'd react to danger. But seeing how he'd handled himself under these extraordinary circumstances inspired deep admiration.

"If you need to talk to someone, I'm here. Or we can get a recommendation for a counselor."

Her gave her hand a squeeze. "Thank you."

She reluctantly stepped back. After she changed out of her uniform and into jeans and a sweater, they climbed inside his truck.

"Why did you come back early?" He fiddled with the heater vents.

"Silver and Mason got called to assist on an assault. Cruz and I had already made our rounds, so we decided to come on in." She buckled her seat belt. "You had the situation under control, though."

"She didn't put up much of a fight when I grabbed her gun. Shock was already setting in." His brow knitted. "I'm angry that more students have gotten swept up in Leonard's destruction. University faculty have a responsibility to them. We're there to guide them in the right direction, offer support and give advice."

"I feel that way when I see parents neglecting or mistreating their children. Or worse, dragging them into a life of crime. We do what we can, what the law allows us to do. Leonard and Desmond will face the music, one way or another. Ultimately, it's in the Lord's hands."

Aiden tuned the radio to a station devoted to eighties music. The ride to Abbott-Craig was uneventful. On campus, they donned sunglasses and caps and joined the stream of people on the sidewalks. They'd gotten a copy of Kelvin's schedule, so they made their way to the communications building and waited outside his classroom. But he didn't show, and the professor confirmed he skipped class.

"Think he'll show at football practice?" she asked Aiden.

"Let's go find out."

He led the way to the football stadium. Although it was a brisk day, the sky was clear and the sun offered comforting warmth. She was examining the passersby, thinking how blessed they were to be getting an education, when Aiden veered off the sidewalk and headed through the short grass toward a pond ringed with trees and benches.

"Aiden?"

He stopped on the high knoll and gazed down at the opaque green water, hands sunk deep into his jacket pockets. His expression was wistful, as if he'd been offered a platter of sweets but couldn't accept.

"What is it?"

"Remember me telling you about the walk on water contest?"

"You organized it during your first year, and the students loved it."

"I did, too." He smiled. "I tasked my materials and construction class with designing twin boat models they could balance each foot on and use to 'walk' across the pond. I had planned for it to be a onetime project, but word got around, and the second semester students begged to do it. It became a tradition. People outside of the architecture department gathered to watch the fun. I became known as the W.O.W. professor. Walk on Water."

Chuckling, he shook off the memories and, taking hold of her elbow, guided her back to the sidewalk. Raven hoped he got to teach again. He poured his all into it, and the architecture program had a hole that only he could fill.

At the stadium, they cut through a cavernous corridor to get to the field. The players were assembling in the middle to do their warm-up stretches. Coaches with whistles around their necks chatted in a cluster of purple shirts and track pants.

"I don't see him."

Another player entered the field and jogged past. "Excuse me." Aiden lifted his hand. "We're looking for Kelvin Farley. Have you seen him?"

"He was right behind me."

Raven turned and spotted Kelvin breezing out of the exit tunnel, his confident stride indicating nothing was amiss in his world. He surely had no idea where his girlfriend was at the moment. She and Aiden started his way. He halted when he saw them, unease shifting through his eyes.

He tightened his grip on the helmet at his thigh. "What do you want?"

"Information," Raven supplied. "But first, you should know that Esme has been arrested."

His jaw sagged. Snapped into place again. "I don't believe you."

"She tried to kill me not more than an hour ago. Are you missing a 9mm, by chance?"

His nostrils flared, and he retreated a step.

"You're spouting lies, man. Esme doesn't know the first thing about guns."

"Happily for me," Aiden responded. "Otherwise, I doubt I'd be standing here talking to you."

Kelvin's handsome features clouded, and he gestured with his helmet. "Whatever. You can leave now. I've got practice."

"You don't seem to understand that you're heading the same place as Esme," Raven said. "She implicated you in Jay's murder. Said you've been Leonard's right-hand man, and that you were with him when Jay was killed. I'm thinking you've had a starring role in our recent close calls." Kelvin's face got paler and paler, the boyish freckles like ink splatters on paper. "You were the one who attacked us in the Ferrers' home. You tried to shoot and then suffocate Aiden in the national park. You were with Leonard when he ran us off the road, and you hunted us through the night."

His Adam's apple bobbed. "You're wrong, lady."

A disgusted noise vibrated in Aiden's throat. "It's Officer Hart, not *lady*."

Raven held out her hand. "Cooperate with us, Kelvin, and I'll make sure you get a deal. Tell us everything, starting with where Leonard is holed up."

Kelvin retreated another step, tossed his helmet at their heads and spun on his heel.

"Wait!"

He raced for the first set of stairs he came to, pounding up the treads and zipping past a cluster of seats. Raven and Aiden gave chase. Kelvin ignored her orders to stop.

At the end of the row, he chose not to descend onto the field again but to go up. He'd trained on the steep concrete stairs, and his legs pumped with ease, carrying him skyward.

Raven had only thought she had stamina—the elliptical hadn't prepared her for this. But she couldn't let him get away. He was too valuable to their case.

Aiden unexpectedly split off, sprinting along a row toward the outer side stairs and then surging upward. Kelvin continued on his path, unaware they were boxing him in. Raven blocked the stairs that would take him to the top tier. He jerked at the sight of Aiden. Spinning, he started to barrel straight for her, only to skid to a stop.

Raven recognized the panic overtaking him. She'd seen it before. He wasn't thinking about anything other than escape, no matter the method.

"Kelvin, listen to me. I know you're upset, but we're going to talk through this, all right?"

Sweat rolled down his face. His chest heaved,

and his eyes reminded her of an untamed horse. He was going to do something drastic.

"I can't go to jail."

The next few moments happened so fast she could hardly process them. Kelvin climbed over the guardrail and began sidestepping toward the juncture of this section and the higher tier.

Aiden curved his hands around the rail and peered over, judging the distance to the ground. Then he looked at Kelvin. Raven's heart leaped into her throat. Surely he wasn't going to climb after him?

"Aiden." Her voice cracked like a whip. "Don't."

A cry ripped from Kelvin as he lost his grip and fell through the air. Gasping, Raven raced to the edge, expecting to see his mangled body on the concrete below.

Aiden's chest constricted, and he had to fight the urge to leap down and help Kelvin. He'd landed on a maintenance platform several stories down. His groans indicated he was alive, but he wasn't moving. His right leg was twisted in an awkward angle.

Raven was already in contact with Dispatch requesting medical assistance and rescue personnel. The coaches and players, who'd watched the dramatic scene unfold, now hurried to join them.

Raven held out her arms, as if she could waylay the entire group herself.

"Stay back, please." Her voice rang with authority as she introduced herself. "The best thing you can do for your teammate is return to the locker rooms and give him the privacy he deserves. Help is on the way. My friend and I will stay here with him until they arrive."

An assistant coach asked to stay, as the head coach was at an appointment and running late. He would expect someone on staff to stick around. Raven agreed, but remained in place until everyone else had left.

Fire trucks and the rescue squad arrived before the EMTs. They devised a way to reach Kelvin from the ground. Aiden held his breath as they lowered him down on a special backboard using a system of ropes and pulleys. The ambulance had arrived by then, and the medics loaded him inside.

Raven sighed. "I pray he makes it."

"Me, too." Despite his role in their troubles, Aiden didn't want the kid to suffer. He was another pawn of Leonard's.

"Let's go down there," she said. "The officers will want to talk to us."

The assistant coach returned to his team waiting inside the stadium locker rooms as Raven and Aiden went in search of the officer in charge. He recognized Officer Kent from the night Leonard had chased them into the gym.

When they approached, his brows crashed together and his eyes narrowed.

"You two again?"

"Officer Kent." Raven inclined her head. "This incident is related to the other night's call. Leonard Grunberg is the source of the trouble."

"We spoke to Leonard that night. He denied your account and provided an alibi."

"By Desmond Whitlock, I know. Convenient, considering he and Leonard share the same goal, which is to silence us."

"Silence you? I'm obviously missing the larger picture. Fill me in."

Raven complied. Officer Kent showed varying levels of shock. As a member of the university police department, he likely didn't encounter this type of criminal complication very often, if ever.

He recorded everything in a small notebook. As his questions tapered off, another officer approached and explained the university chancellor had arrived and was demanding answers. A diminutive woman with big, bouncy hair strode forward—Uma Douglas. Aiden knew her as a force of nature with a seemingly endless supply of drive and energy. Her laser-focused gaze shifted from Officer Kent to flick over Raven and Aiden in dismissal. But then she took a second look at him. And a third.

Her feet tangled beneath her, and she would've pitched forward if not for Kent's quick reflexes. She quickly righted herself and brushed him off, edging closer to Aiden.

"Aiden Ferrer?"

He inclined his head. "Hello, Uma."

"You're dead." Her gaze roamed his face for so long he started to get uncomfortable.

"It's a long and complicated story, but one you need to hear as it involves criminal activity among your employees."

"Excuse me?"

Officer Kent slipped away and left Aiden and Raven to deal with Uma. He relayed the entire time line of events, aware he was hammering the final nails in his professional coffin. This story, once it got out, would affect a lot of people: Leonard, Desmond and other faculty members who'd potentially participated in the cheating ring. The students who'd paid their way through the programs. Those students' parents, some of whom shelled out large amounts of tuition dollars. The townspeople who eagerly supported the school and sports teams would be disappointed. Future students would think twice before coming to a school with a tarnished reputation, especially athletes. Aiden doubted he'd be welcomed back into the Abbott-Craig fold with open arms.

Uma's face pinched into prune-like lines. "You should've come to me with this information right away." She glanced past Aiden and scowled. "The news channel is already here. I've got to do damage control. Don't talk to the media."

She swept herself off, bearing down on the cameraman and reporter.

"I almost feel sorry for them," Raven muttered.

"She can be overbearing at times, but she wants what's best for the university. Not that I have to worry about that. She confirmed what I already suspected. Abbott-Craig is no place for whistleblowers."

"They would be fools to let you go. I'm sure there are other universities who would applaud your actions."

"None of them anywhere close to Morganton or Serenity. I'd have to start over somewhere else."

Raven's expression shuttered. "Maybe that wouldn't be such a bad thing."

He averted his gaze so she wouldn't see his pain. Even if he did have a future to offer her, she'd just made it clear their breakup was permanent.

EIGHTEEN

After leaving the scene, Raven and the rest of the mounted police unit converged on Desmond's house. Silver had apprised his friend in the Morganton Police Department, Detective Blake Jenkins, of recent developments. Jenkins was ready to take the information to his lieutenant and seek to reopen Jay's case. First, however, he planned to take Desmond in for questioning.

Aiden prayed justice would prevail. He stayed in the truck, observing Raven and the others approaching the front door.

Aiden had no aspirations to be in law enforcement, but sitting on the sidelines wasn't pleasant, especially when Raven was a prime target.

Camille opened the door, her manner flustered and confused, and reluctantly allowed Detective Jenkins and Mason to enter. Silver went around back, while Cruz ambled toward the garages. Raven remained on the stoop. They were prepared for Desmond to put up a fight, and Aiden couldn't picture the distinguished department head doing something like that.

It wasn't long before Raven returned to the car and slid into the driver's seat. "According to Mrs. Whitlock, Desmond is traveling out of town for a conference. Something about a society for historical architecture."

"He's running."

"He probably heard what happened to Kelvin. His buddy, Leonard, is in the wind. The sights have switched to him. Jenkins and his team are going to the airport to intercept him. They've already contacted TSA. He'll keep us updated. Once he and his team have a chance to interview Desmond, they'll loop us in."

Aiden stared at the house, where Camille conversed with Mason and Silver. She clutched her sweater at the throat, her face stamped in disbelief. Yet another victim of this whole mess.

"He was leaving her for good," Aiden surmised. "To deal with the fallout of his crimes— shoulder the embarrassment, media attention and financial loss."

"I'll reach out to her in the coming days."

He turned his head to look at her. "If anyone can relate, it's you."

"I wasn't comparing her situation with mine. Desmond left her in order to save his own hide and avoid jail time. Your only thought was to protect me." Her phone buzzed, and she sighed.

"What is it?"

"My mom. She's insisting I come see her tonight. If I don't, she'll park herself in my driveway until I get home. Do you mind the pit stop? You could ride with Mason to his house, and I'll pick you up after."

Leave her alone? Not going to happen. "I don't mind."

"Fair warning, she's not happy with you."

Brenda Hart hadn't hidden the fact that she didn't want him for her daughter. He wasn't sure what she didn't like about him and Raven as a couple. Was she projecting her own relationship failures onto him? Did he remind her of a former boyfriend? Or, like Raven, did she have issues with his chosen profession?

Brenda had lived in the same house for decades. Located deep in the mountain coves, miles from the center of town, it sat like a weathered gray stone upon a steep, unfriendly perch. The gravel driveway was pitted with dips that rocked the car from side to side.

In contrast, the interior was a nest of bold hues that defied the bleak winter beyond its walls— patterned blankets thrown over overstuffed chairs, fat pillows tucked in the couch corners, pottery dishes arranged on the table. The air was scented with cinnamon and nutmeg, which he traced to the platter of cookies on the kitchen counter.

Brenda enveloped her daughter in a hug. "I've been worried about you, sweetheart."

Raven eased out of the embrace. "I'm fine, Mom."

Brenda glared at Aiden while speaking to Raven. "You were shot. How many years have you been a police officer, and this is the first time you've gotten shot? It's because of *him*."

"We've got it under control."

"Hello, Brenda." Aiden inclined his head. "How have you been?"

In answer, she arched a brow at him. Like her daughter, Brenda had luxurious, thick black hair and sun-kissed skin. Her eyes were a darker brown, and she wore her hair lopped off at the shoulders.

Brenda huffed and wagged her finger at Aiden. "You broke my daughter's heart, you and your parents with your fancy degrees and condescending ways."

"Mom."

A frown tugged at his lips. "Are you referring to the retirement party? I'm mortified that my mother acted that way. I've apologized to Raven, and I extend my heartfelt apology to you, as well."

"Not just the party. Her childhood was marked with adversity. She was made to question her self-worth and value because she didn't learn the same way as other students. She rose above it and achieved her dreams, only to be made to feel inferior by the Ferrer family."

His heart thundered against his ribs, and he sought Raven's gaze. "Did I truly make you feel that way?"

"It's not in you to do that to anyone, Aiden. Your parents, on the other hand, were not as gracious."

"I had no idea." His middle knotted. How could he have missed the signs? "I would've put a stop to it. I will speak to them."

"It's behind us, Aiden. I've put it out of my mind." Gauging by her subdued expression, it was obvious she hadn't.

Brenda set the cookie platter on the table with a thunk. "Sit. I'll prepare tea."

When Aiden hesitated, Raven waved him to the end chair. "Better do what she says," she murmured, not meeting his gaze.

"Should you observe in case she decides to poison mine?" he whispered.

Her warm honey eyes shot up in surprise, and he was rewarded with a slight smile. "The cookies might be suspect, too."

They chose seats opposite each other, and

Raven took one cookie for herself and lifted the platter. "Do you dare?"

He snatched one. "I remember your mom's cookies. They're worth the risk."

Soft, rich chocolate melted on his tongue, quickly chased by delicate spices. "Don't tell Greta and Gwyn, but I think these rival their chocolate cake."

Brenda set an orange teapot on the table, along with three mugs. Although unhappy with him, she wouldn't neglect her hostess duties.

"What are you planning to do about Lindsey's wedding?" Brenda demanded. "Hope his trouble doesn't follow you to the church?"

Raven poured steaming, caramel-colored liquid into their mugs. "Silver's arranged for off-duty officers and private security."

Brenda's dark eyes speared Aiden. "Expensive."

He met her gaze. "I've promised to reimburse him." As soon as he secured a job and a place to live, he'd start paying Silver.

She sniffed in disdain.

Raven sighed. "Silver doesn't expect repayment."

"I wouldn't feel right not doing it."

"You have no problem putting my daughter in danger."

"Mom, what did the doctor say about your

ankle?" Raven's nail beds went white as she gripped the mug. "You don't need surgery, I hope."

Brenda pressed her lips together into a thin line. After a time, she shook her head. "I've strained it, that's all. I'll have to take a break from my walking club for a few weeks."

Raven continued to direct the conversation toward safer topics. Their stay lasted a very long half hour before her phone buzzed. She read the text and, shoving the phone into her jacket pocket, pushed the chair back.

"We have to go, Mom. I'll see you at the wedding."

Brenda stood, as well, and wrapped her daughter in another hug. She was happy to bid Aiden goodbye and probably hoped he didn't darken her doorstep again. Once inside the truck, he studied her shadowed profile.

"I never gave much thought to the fact that neither of our families supported our relationship."

"Apparently they saw obstacles we didn't."

"I disagree."

"Our parents want the best for us." Her words were heavy. Sad. "Let's face it, Aiden, we aren't good for each other."

Raven cringed each time she replayed last night's conversation. *Not good for each other?*

Her mind rebelled against the hasty words that rang with falsehood. They shared faith in Jesus and common interests, goals and values. If she disregarded her ingrained insecurities—and that was a huge ask—she'd admit they were actually a great team.

The alarm clock feature chimed again. Scooting up in bed, she positioned her pillows behind her back, unplugged her phone from the charger and read her messages. Desmond had been snatched up by airport security moments before boarding a plane to Rio. After being delivered into Detective Jenkins's custody, he'd been transported to Morganton PD and questioned for hours. He had crooned like a canary, spilling crucial details that Esme didn't have and Kelvin couldn't give, considering he was in the intensive care unit under sedation.

Like Aiden, Desmond had stumbled upon Leonard's scheme. Leonard had offered him a cut of his earnings in exchange for his silence. Desmond had agreed, partly because he was afraid of Leonard and partly because he made some unwise purchases and could funnel extra money to his debt.

Thanks to Desmond's testimony, MPD had reopened Jay's case. They were also sending more uniforms into the community to hunt for Leonard. Raven examined the local news station websites. Any day now, she expected to see the scandal splashed across social media. She wished Aiden could be spared that misery. He'd endured—and sacrificed—so much already in his quest for truth.

A text came through from Silver. She immediately abandoned her cozy cocoon and changed into pants and a long-sleeved unit shirt. Tucking the ends into her waistband as she left her bedroom, she went to wake Aiden. But the couch was empty, the pillow stacked neatly on the folded blankets.

"Aiden?"

A frisson of unease zipped down her spine, and she almost turned back for her weapon. The smell of coffee lured her to the kitchen. Stationed before the fridge, his hands cupping a Smoky Mountains mug, he stared intently at their photograph. His hair was adorably rumpled and his jaw darkened with scruff. His plaid shirt molded to his lean form. Beneath it, he wore a plain white T-shirt over his jeans.

Raven released the air her lungs kept prisoner, but her heartbeat remained sluggish. Her feet threatened to carry her forward, her arms aching to slip around his waist. She yearned to burrow into his chest and absorb his warmth, his steadfastness, his ready affection.

He continued to contemplate the photo. "We

were good together, Raven." His words were scraped up from within, and his tone dared her to disagree.

Raven didn't know what to say. What would agreeing with him accomplish? And yet, she sensed he was seeking a confrontation.

"We have to go." She waited for him to focus on her before continuing. "Leonard's been sighted at a gas station not far from here. You and I will meet Silver there while Cruz and Mason man the stables."

"I want to hear you say it."

She tilted her head to one side, and her hair rippled into her face. She impatiently shoved it behind her ear. "Fine. We were good together. Fantastic, in fact."

"Breaking up was a mistake."

"No, Aiden. You and I shouldn't have gotten together in the first place. I should've heeded my initial gut reaction and spared us both a lot of heartache."

His forehead creased. "But you just said—"

"If I'd had a different childhood..." Raven fought to suppress the shame that accompanied those elementary and middle school memories. "I have too much baggage to ever truly be comfortable as your partner."

His mouth slanted with anger. "We all have baggage, Raven. We have assets and shortcomings. God made us each unique, with specific talents and abilities. You're good at things I wouldn't even attempt. We struggle with different issues. None of us are one hundred percent capable. We're all a little damaged in one way or another." His eyes swirled with anger beneath lowered brows. "I'm not trying to convince you to give us another chance. That ship has sailed. We're in very different places from where we were a year ago. But it makes me angry when you sell yourself short. You can be with whoever you want. Brain surgeon. Engineer. Airplane pilot. Janitor. Car salesman. Be with someone you like and respect as a man, irrespective of his professional label." He reached behind him, snagged her monogrammed travel mug and held it out without a word. "Let's go get Leonard. Then we can finally move on with our lives."

He brushed past her as he left the room, unaware he'd just slayed her with his words.

NINETEEN

The attack came out of nowhere. A *thwump* preceded the explosion of glass, and everyone inside the gas station dived to the floor. Ears ringing, Aiden shielded Raven with his body in anticipation of whatever came next. She twisted onto her side and whipped out her weapon, her eyes shooting off angry sparks.

"Text Silver."

"On it." Aiden fired off the text and received an almost immediate response. "He's five minutes out."

Sticking close to the wall, she hustled toward the gaping hole, wedging between the long counter and a sunglasses display. Before he could form his next thought, bullets sprayed inside. Screams interspersed the destruction of paper, metal and glass housed in the aisles. Aiden began to herd the customers—a pair of older men in overalls, a thirtyish businesswoman and a uniformed delivery truck driver—behind the counter where the clerk had taken cover. The stack of two-liter sodas beside him erupted, spewing liquid. One bottle flew up to the ceiling, bounced off and whacked his head.

"Aiden?" Raven called out.

"I'm good."

The onslaught ceased. But for how long was anyone's guess. Into the metallic silence came soft, keening cries. His chest tightened. Sidling closer to the rear aisle, he spotted a teenage girl seated by the chips, knees hugged to her chest and rocking side to side.

He extended his hand. "Are you hurt?"

She didn't respond. Aiden gauged the open gap between him and the metal display to be about three feet. He couldn't leave her there.

"Raven?" He could only see her shoulder and sneaker. "I'm going to cross to the other end of the store. Someone needs my help."

"I don't have eyes on him," she tersely responded. "I think he's behind the Dumpsters, but there's a semi and a storage shed jammed on either side. I can't be sure he hasn't moved locations."

If Leonard circled around to the rear exit, he and the teenager would be vulnerable. At least if everyone was behind the cash register, Raven could switch positions and provide protection.

"I'll be quick."

"I'm holding you to that."

Aiden lunged across the gap, landing on his stomach beside the bubble gum selection. Leonard must've noted the movement, because another round of deadly bullets streamed inside. The refrigerated cases along the back wall popped and splintered. More screams assaulted his ears, and he crawled toward the teenager.

When it let up, he thanked God neither one of them had gotten hit by a ricochet. He heard Raven interacting with the clerk, who gave a report of himself and the others.

"Hey there, I'm Aiden. What's your name?" When she didn't respond, he lightly touched her arm.

She flinched, but she did make eye contact. Her mascara ran in rivulets down her face, and she was even younger than he'd thought at first—thirteen or fourteen at the most.

"What's your name?" he repeated.

"H-Holly."

"Nice to meet you, Holly. You live near here?"

She blinked at the innocuous question. "Three streets over."

"So you walked here? Biked? Or maybe you have a moped?"

She stopped rocking. "I—I have a bicycle."

"Where did you park it?"

"Under the tree." She hooked her thumb to indicate the left side of the parking lot.

"Great choice." In that out-of-the-way spot, the bicycle was probably exactly how she left it. "Holly, I need you to come with me. We're going behind the register with the others."

Fear resurged in her eyes. "I want to stay here."

He opened his mouth to respond, but Raven cut him off, wanting a status report.

"We're good back here. Any sign of Silver?" Surely the five minutes had passed already.

"Negative."

Holly sniffed and wiped her cheeks. "Is that lady a cop?"

He smiled. "A very brave and capable one."

"Are you?"

"No, I'm a teacher."

A clanging sound reached him from the back of the store near the restrooms. He couldn't see the door, but he heard it open and slam shut. Heard the heavy, determined tread of footsteps. Silver wouldn't enter unannounced. He wouldn't enter the store at all until he'd secured the suspect's location. There was only one explanation.

Raven was already yelling his name. Holly gasped. Aiden leaped to his feet, seized her arms and hauled her up. "Go!"

He propelled Holly toward the counter, not sparing precious seconds to peer behind him.

Raven skidded past them, careening around the corner and ordering Leonard to drop his weapon.

Aiden shoved Holly to safety, hustling in the crowded space behind her and searching for a weapon of any sort that he could use to assist Raven. His gaze caught on the curved mirror attached to the ceiling, and he saw Leonard level his gun at her chest. Denial roared through him. Spinning, he lunged back into the store in time to hear her fire her weapon.

A shocked howl rocked Leonard as blood spurted from his hand. His gun slipped to the floor, and he sprinted back the way he'd come.

Aiden squeezed her shoulder. "You all right?"

She jerked a nod. "You?"

"Scratches and bruises."

"The others?" Her gaze flicked to the cash register.

"Holly's fine. Everyone else, as well."

"Stay with them?"

He nodded. "Of course."

She was running after Leonard before he finished answering, the debris crunching beneath her boots. He would never get used to watching her run into danger. Would probably have nightmares about it. He prayed that the Lord would put a hedge of protection around her. Through the uneven gaps in the windows, he saw Silver's

Corvette zoom into the lot and squeal to a stop by the pumps.

The clerk popped up. "I'm out of here."

The two men also stood. Aiden retraced his steps, careful not to slip in the spilled soda. "It's not safe yet. We have to stay put until the police give the all clear."

The trio grumbled. Ignoring them, Aiden rounded the counter. "How are you doing, Holly?"

She frowned and shrugged. He spotted a box of tissues on the shelves beneath the register and handed them to her. She slowly mopped her face.

Sirens pierced the morning, and a horde of police cruisers surrounded the building. He felt a jerk on his sleeve, and he looked down to find Holly standing close.

"I'm going to get into trouble. I ditched school."

"The police are here to arrest the shooter. Trust me, the important thing is you're unharmed." She bit her lip, probably unaware that she still had a death grip on his sleeve. "I'm curious. Why didn't you go to school?"

"It's a waste of time."

Aiden studied her youthful face and recognized the shame and self-doubt reflected in her eyes. She was having trouble learning, but she didn't know who to reach out to for help. Before he could respond, Officer Bell entered the building and began interviewing them. Sheriff's deputies arrived on scene, and Holly slipped out while Aiden was giving his statement. She paused at the door to give him a sort of salute, then hurried away. Raven and Silver returned then... Without Leonard.

His stomach churned. When Raven strode inside, her expression reflected his own disappointment and frustration. Her frown became more pronounced as she cataloged the destruction.

"What happened?"

She shook her head. "He slipped through our fingers again. He's injured, though, and that will slow him down. We're putting all our resources into locating him." Taking his hand in her smaller one, she squeezed. "I'm grateful no one got hurt. You were amazing."

"I didn't do anything. You're the one who fended him off."

"You got everyone to safety so I could focus on doing my job. Thank you."

He gingerly grazed her cheek with his fingertips. "I'm sorry about earlier. I shouldn't have pressed you. The truth is, I care about you and always will. I want you to be healthy and happy. I hope that, when this is all over, we can remain friends."

It wasn't ideal, but he couldn't live with resentment or unresolved issues between them.

Her eyes got misty. She nodded. "I know, Aiden. I want the same for you."

He lowered his hand to his side, feeling as though he'd lost the only thing that mattered in life.

Their usual patrols had to be suspended for the day, so they released the horses into the paddock. Mason remained at the stables and called area hospitals and clinics in hopes Leonard had sought medical treatment. Raven, Aiden, Silver and Cruz paid visits to his usual haunts, starting with his favored gun range and ending with his girlfriend's workplace. No one was willing to part with information. His survivalist buddies were skeptical of law enforcement, and his ex-wife and girlfriend seemed to be protecting themselves against his potential wrath and retaliation.

By the end of her shift, Raven had a pounding headache. Aiden brought her a banana, granola bar and caffeinated soda from the break room. "I couldn't locate the pain reliever. Caffeine might help."

He'd always been good at anticipating her needs. "Is paying attention to details a prerequisite for architects?"

He smiled. "It helps."

The fizzy drink felt good against her dry throat.

"You should go home and catch up on sleep."

"Can't." She twisted the cap back on. "I've got wedding favor duty tonight, remember?"

"Lindsey will understand your absence after the day you've had. She has Thea and the others to help her."

"It's not about the extra set of hands. As her friend and bridesmaid, I'm supposed to share in her happy day and the traditions and tasks that go along with it."

"What about Leonard?"

"Silver and Mason have offered to stand watch. Weiland will accompany you to my house."

His brows lowered. "I'd prefer to stick together."

"I assumed you'd want to rest."

"I can rest when Leonard is behind bars."

Raven experienced a pang of trepidation. She worried that Leonard had fled the area, possibly even the state. He could have out-of-state friends willing to give him sanctuary until the heat died down. If that happened, neither she nor Aiden could fully lower their guard. Normal life would be a mere fantasy.

She waved her hand down her dirty, sticky clothes. "I have to stop by the house and change first. There will be food at Silver's. Saves us from worrying about supper."

An hour and a half later, she and Aiden arrived at Silver's house.

"If you can't tell from the noise level," he said to her, "they're in the office."

The long kitchen island was covered with appetizers, sandwiches and salads. White candles in silver cylinders dotted the kitchen and living area. Mason was already filling his plate. He nodded to Aiden. "Lindsey gave us permission to eat whenever we were ready. Help yourself."

"Don't mind if I do." He turned to Raven. "What about you?"

"I'll check in with the girls first."

Aiden joined Mason at the island, and they began to converse.

Silver pulled Raven aside. "I want to show you something." Retrieving a velvet box from his pocket, he popped it open. "A surprise for Lindsey. I'm going to give them to her before the ceremony. Or on our honeymoon. I haven't decided. What do you think?"

Raven admired the diamond-and-ruby earrings. "They're perfect."

His smile was as bright as the candlelight. "Red's her favorite color."

She went on tiptoe and kissed his cheek. He looked dumbfounded. "What was that for?"

"I'm happy for you, my friend. For both of you."

He returned the box to his pocket. "Can I give you a piece of advice?"

"Do I have a choice?"

"You and Aiden were good together. You obviously still care about each other. If there's any way to make it work, do it. If I had let the past dictate my future, I wouldn't be about to marry Lindsey."

Raven glanced at Aiden. His impassioned speech that morning had gotten her thinking. Was he right? Was she selling herself short because a select group of students and teachers had labeled her as less than? Thoughts churning, she descended the stairs to the bottom level and entered the spacious office.

The girls greeted her from their workstation at the foldaway table. Lindsey jumped up to greet her. Clad in black pants and a snug red sweater with tiny white hearts, her hair skimming her cheeks, she shone with happiness.

"Silver told me everything." She bit her lip. "Raven, I've been thinking. With everything going on, maybe we should postpone the wedding."

"Absolutely not." Raven took her friend's hands in hers. "First of all, Silver would have a meltdown. The man is practically giddy with anticipation, a state that could only be caused by you and this great big love he has for you." Behind the red-framed glasses, Lindsey's big brown eyes got shiny. "Secondly, I would never forgive myself if I caused a delay. Everything is set. The caterer. The preacher. Flowers. Photography. Doughnut wall."

At that, Lindsey giggled. "Believe it or not, that was Silver's idea."

"He can't stop raving about the bacon maple doughnut you guys sampled." She laughed. "This from a guy who never used to eat sweets. You've corrupted him, Linds."

"My favorite is the red velvet doughnut. And yeah, I guess I have." Her gaze got starry. "I can't believe I get to be his wife, Raven."

"This wedding will go on as scheduled, even if I have to stand at the door myself in my brides-maid gown and my 9mm instead of a bouquet."

TWENTY

"Dare I ask what's on your mind?"

Raven waved to Officer Weiland—seated in his cruiser in the driveway—and inserted the key into the lock. Despite being bone-tired, her mood was lighter than it had been in days. A few hours spent with Lindsey, Thea and the other women, focused on something other than keeping Aiden safe, had been an unexpected blessing. They'd eaten good food and chatted about the wedding. The normal activity had been so nice, she hadn't thought to be sad about her own canceled nuptials.

When she and the others had gone upstairs, Aiden had seemed to be relaxed in Mason's and Silver's company. He hadn't spoken during the ride home, however.

Once inside her kitchen, he shrugged out of his jacket and draped it over the chair back. A hint of stubble darkened his jaw. "The teenager inside the gas station this morning?"

"Holly? What about her?"

"She wasn't in school."

"With everything going on, the fact that it's the middle of the week didn't register. Maybe she's homeschooled?"

"No, I asked her about it." Leaning against the counter, he crossed his arms. "She said school's a waste of time."

"Typical teenager response."

"I sense there's a deeper issue."

His gaze was steady. Penetrating. Understanding dawned. "You think she has an undiagnosed learning disability? That's a big leap to make based on a brief interaction with a stranger. Where are you going with this?"

"Volunteering is important to you. What if you were to direct your efforts in a different area? A place where kids struggling in school could go to get help? No red tape, no hoops to jump through. Helping anyone who walks through the door, no questions asked."

Raven stared at him. "Like a tutoring center? I'm hardly qualified to help anyone learn to read."

"You have firsthand experience of what it's like to want to learn, but even giving your best efforts ends up being futile."

She got choked up. "You mean I know what

it's like to feel dumb. To feel like a failure. That something's wrong with me."

Aiden rounded the table and cupped her shoulders. He looked down into her eyes, his own full of confidence. In her. The fact he'd suggested this amazed her.

"There are many wonderful, insightful, caring teachers in our school system. Still, students sometimes slip through the cracks. What if there was a safe place for them to go, a place they wouldn't be ridiculed or judged, a place that would give them hope?"

"I wish I'd had something like that."

"I suggest you pray about it."

"I will."

Aiden bid her good-night and retreated into the spare bedroom. Raven went through the motions of preparing for bed, her mind bursting with too many subjects. Leonard's location. The wedding on Saturday. Aiden's surprising suggestion.

She lay in bed for what seemed like hours, unable to relax. She had just drifted off when a loud pop ripped her from sleep. Her 9mm was on her nightstand, and she reached for it. Before she could wrap her fingers around it, a burly man busted through the door and lunged for her. Leonard. How had he gotten past Weiland? Was the officer all right? Where was Aiden?

She rolled to the other side of the bed. Thick,

meaty fingers clamped onto the back of her neck. His knee wedged into her spine, pinning her face down. He bound her wrists with what felt like cord. She screamed for Aiden. Terror slithered through her. He would've responded by now if he could have. Had Leonard gotten to him first? Her brain supplied too many graphic scenarios.

"Aiden!"

Fabric was stuffed into her mouth, and she gagged.

Leonard bent over her, his breath foul and his tone gleeful. "You'll be reunited with your professor soon enough."

He hauled her upright and propelled her through the house and out into the night. Her T-shirt and drawstring pajama pants were no match for the cold. Stray gravel ground through her socks and into her sensitive soles.

He directed her toward a truck with a horse trailer attached. As they passed the cruiser, she peered inside. The driver's side window was broken. Weiland was slumped over the wheel, his temple and face bloodied. Unconscious? Or beyond help? *Please, Lord, don't let him be dead.*

She didn't get a chance to dwell on it. Leonard yanked open the truck's rear door with his injured hand. Bloodied gauze was wrapped around it.

"Lay down on the seat," he growled, shoving her inside.

Her feet tangled in a pair of legs sprawled across the footwell. Aiden! His wrists were bound, like hers. He didn't react to her arrival. She fell across the seat and peered over the edge. His eyes were closed. Was he breathing?

Because her hands were tied behind her back and the gag prevented her from speaking, she used her feet to jostle his. Her heart threatened to beat out of her chest when he didn't respond. Didn't stir.

She nudged him harder, over and over until he shifted and groaned.

Tears leaked from the corners of her eyes. *Thank you, Lord.*

"Raven?" His voice was rough with pain.

Leonard climbed behind the wheel, and the engine roared to life. She prayed for God to make a way for their deliverance. It was the middle of the night. No one would miss Weiland for hours. By the time anyone figured out something was amiss, they would be long gone. It was up to her and Aiden to save themselves. But how?

Panic—like the kind she'd experienced when asked to write a paper or give a speech, only worse—darkened her mind. Muddled her thoughts. She prayed for a clear head.

Based on what she knew about Leonard, and the fact he'd brought horses, suggested he was taking them somewhere remote, somewhere he could finish them off without fear of interference. Then he'd take his time disposing of their bodies.

Movement below caught her eye, and she saw Aiden attempting to sit up. She nudged his legs with her foot and shook her head. He seemed to understand, because he eased back down. A passing streetlight flickered over his face, and she made a sound deep in her throat. Blood glistened in his hair and had dried on his temple and cheek.

Leonard heard her. "Might as well accept that I've won, Officer Hart. At least you and the professor will be together."

She locked gazes with Aiden. Were these their final moments?

His head throbbed with each heartbeat. He'd been asleep when Leonard entered his room and had woken up a split second before he'd been struck by a blunt object. His back burned and his shoulders were sore, indicating Leonard had dragged him out of the house and across the driveway. He must've secured his wrists before stuffing him inside the truck. All this with a wounded hand. The man was tough as nails. A formidable foe.

Would Leonard finally carry out his goal? He had nothing to lose, at this point. Why stop short of ending his enemies' lives?

Lord Jesus, remind me of Your promises. To

never leave or forsake us. To give us a future and hope.

He squeezed his eyes shut. *Your thoughts are above mine, Lord. I don't know how this is going to end, but I know Your way is the best way.*

He thought of the missteps he'd made in this situation, starting with the first discovery of cheating more than a year ago. More excruciating were the mistakes he'd made with Raven.

I would ask, Father, that You please spare her. She shouldn't have to pay the price for my actions. I love her. I always will.

His feelings hadn't faded with time or distance. He was more in love with her now than he ever was.

The truck hit a pothole, and Raven almost rolled off the seat and onto him. Leonard swerved, and she wiggled away from the edge. He wished he could ask her if she was hurt. Or if she knew what had happened to Officer Weiland.

Fury started low in his belly and, as the miles slipped past, built into a furious blaze. He had no weapon, and his hands were literally tied, but he was determined not to go out without a fight.

The streetlights became less frequent, and they eventually turned onto an uneven surface. Was this the national park? A buddy's isolated property?

Leonard stopped the truck, and Aiden's body

tensed. He opened the rear passenger door and pulled Raven out by her feet.

"I'll be back to deal with you."

"No. Take me first—"

The door slammed shut, and Aiden started yelling. He maneuvered to a sitting position and felt a wave of nausea, which he ignored. Tugging on the cord only served to dig it deeper into his flesh. Leonard didn't return, so Aiden closed his mouth and tried to detect any sound at all from Raven. He felt the truck shift slightly, followed by the clump of horse hooves on the trailer floor. Leonard was unloading the horses... For a ride into the backcountry, no doubt. The tension in his body relaxed ever so slightly. They had a reprieve.

Aiden used his elbows to leverage himself onto the stiff leather seat. The truck beams cut swaths into the darkness. Raven stood near the truck, warily watching Leonard's movements—they were safe for the moment.

He brought out two unsaddled horses. Then he removed Raven's gag and sliced through her restraint.

"Climb on."

"What are you doing, Leonard?" she demanded. "Killing a law enforcement officer carries stiff penalties."

"Shut up, and do what I tell you. Or I can gag you again."

She walked around to the first horse's side and hauled herself onto its back.

"Good girl. Stay put, you hear? Remember what I said. You cooperate, and I won't make the professor suffer."

Leonard greeted Aiden with a grunt. Once he was out of the truck, his wrists freed, Leonard ordered him to ride with Raven. She held out her arm to give him a boost. He made it on the second try, carefully wrapping his arms around her middle.

"You okay?" he whispered against her ear.

In answer, she covered his hand with hers and squeezed tightly.

Leonard mounted his horse and pointed his weapon at them. "Let's go."

As they left the truck behind, Raven spoke. "Where are we, Leonard?"

"Hardly matters."

"I'm wondering how easy it will be for you to evade the police. Your image is being circulated on social media and the news. The evidence is already stacked against you. Your friend Desmond spilled his guts. Esme has become very chatty, and Kelvin will likely take a deal once he's coherent enough to make that decision. Killing us will make life much harder for you, you know.

You'll be hunted with even more intensity. Leave the area now. By the time Aiden and I reach civilization, you could be in another country."

Leonard's silence unnerved Aiden. Was he considering her suggestion?

Raven slowed the horse. "What's it going to be, Leonard? Freedom or revenge?"

He laughed. "Both."

Her body stiffened in the circle of Aiden's arms. "You'll regret that decision."

"Stop talking."

They rode for another mile through rolling pastures dotted with trees. The sky overhead was a curtain of black sprinkled with silver glitter. The air wrapped them in its chilly embrace. Once in a while, a shudder would wrack Raven's body, and Aiden would hold her closer against his chest. He needed to do something to protect her. To spare her. But what?

"She's right, Leonard," he said. "The murder of a police officer won't be taken lightly. You want me, after all. I'm the one who unraveled your operations. Let her go."

Her nails bit into his hand. "Aiden, stop."

"Noble of you, but you've both caused me enormous headaches. Time to dismount."

Raven gave the horse a soft command, and he halted. Aiden slid down to the ground and whirled toward Leonard, who'd already dismounted.

"You're not thinking clearly—"

"You're the one with that issue," Leonard retorted, leveling his gun at Aiden.

"Don't." Raven rushed to Aiden's side, arms outstretched. "Listen to me. I can work out a deal for you—if you leave us unharmed."

"You have very little faith in me. I'm not going to be captured because I'm smarter than Desmond and the others. I'm smarter than law enforcement. I've got a foolproof plan in place and will be sipping cold brews by the lake before your bodies are cold. Now, which one of you goes first?" He pointed the gun at Aiden, then Raven. Back and forth, again and again, like a child's game. "You made me suffer, Professor. It's your turn. Watch as your girlfriend bleeds out and know you can't do a thing to stop it."

Aiden's blood ran cold. He shoved Raven out of the way, lunging to shield her from certain death. Pain ripped through his abdomen. He crumpled to his knees, his hands automatically searching out the wound. They came away wet and sticky. Raven's horrified scream pierced him. She scrambled toward him. Light-headedness washed over him, and he slumped onto his side.

The last thing he saw was her fear-filled face.

TWENTY-ONE

Raven gathered Aiden's limp body in her arms and cradled him close. "Aiden, wake up. Stay with me."

The moon cast enough light for her to make out the dark red stain on his shirt. She pressed one hand on the wound to try to staunch the flow. It was like trying to dam a leak with a toothpick. His head lolled to the side and came to rest against her knee.

She bent and pressed a kiss to his forehead. "Don't leave me again. Please."

"This isn't the way I pictured it," Leonard grumbled. "He can't stop playing hero for a second, can he?"

Raven glared up at him through her tears. "You'll get what's coming to you. Maybe not tonight or next week or even next month. But justice will eventually prevail. My unit won't rest until you've paid for your crimes."

He merely smiled, the embodiment of arrogance, selfishness and evil. He raised his weapon. She deliberately shifted her gaze to Aiden's face. He was the love of her life. She'd go to her grave focused on him and the beauty of what they'd shared together. They'd made plenty of mistakes, but at the heart of it, they were bound together by a deep respect and selfless love.

She stroked his cheek. "I love you."

The blast made her ears ring, and she braced for impact. But no pain registered.

Whipping up her head, she saw Leonard's stunned expression, saw him stumble a few steps to the right before thundering to the ground like a mighty oak disintegrated by lightning. A man emerged from the shadows, running toward them, weapon in hand.

"Cruz!"

When he reached them, his flinty gaze raked over Aiden. "Sorry I wasn't in time to prevent this."

He checked to make sure Leonard was no longer a threat. "He's gone."

"H-how?"

Cruz returned to her side. Kneeling on the ground, he removed and folded his jacket and pressed it against Aiden's wound.

"Weiland stirred long enough to send out a distress call. We responded to the scene and watched his dashcam footage. Once we knew what vehicle to look for, we sent out the BOLO. A deputy spotted you and called it in."

Raven ran her trembling hand over Aiden's hair. "It's bad, Cruz. Isn't it?"

His brown eyes were stark, but his jaw was set. "He's a fighter. He fought his way back to you, didn't he?"

Silver arrived carrying a backboard. His face was like granite as he surveyed the scene. His violet gaze clashed with Raven's, communicating more than words ever could. He and Cruz strapped Aiden in. Raven led the horses while the men carried Aiden back to the road where the truck and trailer were parked.

An ambulance arrived mere minutes after they did, and paramedics took over Aiden's care. Raven asked to ride with him, and they agreed. Cruz and Silver took turns giving her a quick hug.

Cruz handed her an extra jacket from his vehicle. "Put that on. I'll bring you clothes and shoes."

She shrugged on the jacket and climbed into the ambulance.

"I'll stay with the body until the sheriff's department arrives," Silver told her. "Then I'll come to the hospital."

The driver closed the doors, shutting her in with the second paramedic and Aiden. Raven could only watch, helpless, as he received life-saving measures. At the hospital, they whisked him off to surgery and her to an exam room. Her feet were scratched and bruised, but she was otherwise physically fine.

Cruz entered the room while she was waiting to sign paperwork. He placed a duffel bag on the bed beside her and propped his hands on his waist.

"Any word?"

Her throat got thick and her vision blurry. "No."

His astute gaze roamed over her face. He opened his arms in invitation. Raven stepped into them and released her grief and worry.

"The thought of going through it all again... this time for real..."

She'd been so foolish to let others' perceptions of her keep her from love and happiness.

Cruz patted her back. "You will do what you have to do, Raven. You're one of the strongest women I know."

He located a tissue box for her, and she mopped up her tears.

"I'm going to change clothes. Oh, how's Weiland?"

"Concussion and thirty stitches."

"Ouch."

He shrugged. "He'll get a few days off for his trouble."

Raven changed into the clothes and sneakers Cruz had picked up from her house. As soon as the nurse said she was free to go, they made their way to the surgical floor waiting room. Mason and Tessa were already there. After doling out hugs, they prayed with her, thanking God for putting an end to the danger and pleading for Aiden's recovery.

When Silver and Lindsey arrived, she struggled to maintain her composure. "I'm blessed to have you all in my life. I don't know what I'd do without you."

"You won't have to find out," Lindsey vowed. "You're never getting rid of us."

The surgeon entered the waiting room, and Raven tried to gauge his expression. The balance of her life rested on his words.

"He sustained some internal damage, but we were able to make necessary repairs."

"He's going to be okay?"

"I expect him to make a full recovery."

Thank You, Jesus. Raven felt like crying all over again. "When can I see him?"

"He's in post-op care now. Should be moved to a room within the hour."

She thanked the doctor and, turning back to the room, found herself enveloped in a group hug. A sheriff's deputy arrived to take her and Cruz's statements. Then it was finally time to see Aiden.

He was asleep when she entered the room. His black hair was in stark contrast to the white pillow. There were shadows under his eyes and stubble along his jaw. Although hooked to an IV and monitors, he looked peaceful.

She wrapped her fingers around his, grateful to feel their warmth. *Thank You for sparing him, Father. Not once, but twice.* He'd given up everything to try to protect her. He'd almost given his life for her. The love she'd tried to hold back, stuff down and pretend wasn't there refused to be ignored.

He stirred, his head shifting on the pillow and eyes flickering open. "Hey, beautiful."

Raven gave him a tearful smile. "Hey, handsome."

"What happened?"

"You saved my life."

He closed his eyes. "Leonard?"

"He's dead. Wieland alerted Dispatch, which led to them locating the truck. Cruz arrived in time to take him down." She ran her fingers over his knuckles. "It's over, Aiden."

His smile was the most beautiful sight she'd seen in a very long time. "You're safe."

"Thanks to you."

He didn't respond, and after some time, she released his hand and got comfortable in the chair next to his bed. She wasn't leaving his side unless he asked her to. She was finally ready to fight for what she wanted.

When Aiden woke again, he discovered Raven wasn't a figure in a medicine-induced dream. She immediately came to his bedside, her eyes like sparkling topaz.

"How are you feeling?" She tucked the sheet more firmly around him, her movements gentle. "What can I get you? Water? Soda?"

He extended his hand, and she sandwiched it in between hers. "Thank you for staying."

"I'm here for as long as you want me," she rasped, her voice husky with longing. "I'll take you home and nurse you back to health, if you'll let me."

"I'd think you'd be ready for a break from me."

She bit her lip. "Never."

"Never is a long time." He tried to determine if what he saw in her eyes was real or hope fueled by lingering anesthesia.

"I've lost too much time with you already."

He pushed the button to adjust the bed to a more upright position. "What exactly are you saying?"

"I'm sorry I hurt you. I let my past overtake

sound judgment. I finally understand that we're all flawed in different ways, yet God equips us to make this world a better place and point others to Christ. If I'd only fixed my eyes on Jesus instead of my own shortcomings, I would've walked into our future with confidence." She took a fortifying breath. "Is it too late for us, Aiden?"

His heart threatened to jump out of his chest. "I never stopped loving you. You're the woman I want, now and always. Nothing will ever change that. I can't offer you the same life as I did before. I'm currently without a home or job, and I can't promise when or if my career will get back on track."

Leaning over, she cradled his cheek with her hand. "I love you, Aiden. I don't care if you're a dishwasher or a professor." She grinned, and her whole face lit up. "Besides, I happen to own a house big enough for two people…and hopefully a few kids someday."

"Are you saying you're willing to reinstate our engagement?"

"I want to marry you as soon as possible, Dr. Ferrer."

A smile splitting his face, he cupped the back of her head and pulled her close for a kiss.

TWENTY-TWO

"How are you feeling? We don't have to stay for the cake."

Seated beside Aiden at a decorated table near the doughnut wall display, Raven linked her arm with his and studied his face for signs of fatigue or discomfort. Handsome in a three-piece navy suit on loan from Silver, his jet-black waves slicked off his face and his jaw freshly shaven, he didn't look as if he'd had surgery two days prior. He'd been discharged yesterday and, though weak and sore, had insisted on being her date for the wedding.

"Not stay for cake?" His brows shot up. "How dare you even suggest such a thing?"

She glanced at his plate, where half the contents had been left. His appetite hadn't fully returned, and he was taking medicine to manage the pain. He should be on the couch. Once again, he was sacrificing his own comfort for her sake.

"We're going home. I'll task Cruz with bringing us cake."

Seated across the table, Cruz ran a finger beneath his stiff shirt collar. He'd shown up in a spiffy black suit. Silver had probably threatened him not to wear his usual jeans and cowboy boots. He looked up from his phone. "I'll have to charge you a delivery fee."

"Take it home with you, and we'll have something to look forward to tomorrow when Aiden brings his stuff over."

They'd agreed he should find a place to bunk until their own ceremony. Aiden's friend Pete had offered a room, but he lived in Morganton. Aiden had already made contact with a local cabin builder who was interested in having him design cabins. Cruz was the best option if Aiden wanted to stay close to Raven.

"Thanks again for letting me stay," Aiden told him.

"Happy to do it."

"Ready to go?" Raven asked.

Aiden's brow furrowed. "I'm fine. Honestly."

She framed his face with both hands and kissed him. The contact arrowed through her, as it always did, inciting a delightful yearning. "I'm not. I'm exhausted. To be honest, I could stand to take a month's vacation. How about you?"

He smiled, his eyes reflecting joy. "I like that idea."

Cruz grunted. "You two should've gotten married alongside Silver and Lindsey."

Aiden caressed her cheek and flashed a roguish grin. "Why didn't I think of that?"

"I doubt Silver would've agreed to share his day." Raven gently directed his chin and gaze toward the dance floor, where Silver and Lindsey swayed to the music, utterly absorbed in each other.

Silver looked distinguished in his unique gray tuxedo with black shirt and tie, his gray hair styled to perfection. Lindsey's short hair had been curled into ringlets that danced around her dainty face, and she wore her signature red lipstick to match her glasses. Raven was pretty sure the bride hadn't stopped smiling since entering the church in her elegant white dress.

Raven was thrilled for her friends. The celebration had been made even sweeter with her own dear man by her side.

Aiden's gaze returned to her, full of promise. "We'll have our own special day soon enough."

She rested her head on his shoulder and huddled closer. "I can't wait."

EPILOGUE

Aiden soaked in Raven's radiant happiness and thanked God for the umpteenth time for taking their mistakes and turning them into something beautiful. This day was almost as significant as his wedding day, which had taken place nearly two months ago in early April.

Sliding her arms around his waist, she gazed at him with shining eyes. "This wouldn't have been possible without you."

A slight breeze stirred her hair, which rippled over her shoulders in a black curtain. He skimmed the strands behind her ears and braced either side of her neck with his hands.

"We did it together."

"I wouldn't have dared dream of something like this, much less attempted to make it real. Thanks to you, children in Serenity have a safe place to seek answers and get help."

Serenity Literacy and Tutoring Center would open its doors today. As the director, Raven would have a central role in the operations. She'd appointed a team of like-minded people in the educational field to assist her. It would be funded through donations. Thanks to Silver's generous donation, they'd secured a house on the edge of the shopping district zoned for commercial use. Serenity's law enforcement members had chipped in both funds and manual labor to transform the older home into an inviting, cheerful space that would put kids at ease.

"Holly promised she'd come by today," Raven said.

"She'll be here."

They'd located Holly's residence and approached her about giving input for the center. She'd been reluctant at first, but as Raven explained her experiences, Holly had opened up about her own struggles and fears. They'd gotten her tested and, with the help of professionals, made a plan to help her. In turn, she'd helped them view the center from a student's perspective.

"Let's go inside." Grinning like a kid about to enter a candy shop, Raven led the way up the porch stairs and inserted the key into the lock of the arched door.

The interior smelled like a lemon drop. Warm sunshine streamed through the windows, spilling onto the gleaming wood floors, colorful rugs and small seating areas tucked in the nooks and crannies. Aiden stood on the threshold as Raven went around the room, her fingers skimming tables, books on the shelves, containers of pens, markers and crayons. She returned to him and, bracing her hands on his chest, leaned up and kissed him.

"I mean it, Aiden. Thank you. It's going to demand a lot of time and attention in the beginning. My off-duty hours will be busy."

"I know, and I don't mind. When I'm not at work, I'll be here with you. I'm at your command."

"But once classes start in the fall…"

He cupped her cheek. "I don't mind the commute. Truly."

A week after getting shot, he'd had an interview with Tyler Construction and gotten a position designing cabins. His skills had been rusty at first, but he'd soon found his groove and learned he enjoyed the creative outlet. The media storm that descended had been trying, but Raven and his newly expanded circle of friends had helped him navigate the incessant interview requests and reporters lurking about.

The university had reached out to him. Instead of chastising him, they'd offered his old job back, along with a new opportunity. He was to form an early intervention program for first- and second-year students. They would receive study skills, test-taking practice and tutoring help in a variety of areas for free. In a way, he was mirroring Raven's efforts, only at the college level.

He would finish with cabin design and resume his professor mantle in the fall. He and Raven had discussed selling the house in Serenity and moving midway between the towns, but for now, they'd decided to stay put.

Before the wedding, he and Raven had sat down with Brenda and his parents and had a difficult but fruitful discussion. His mom had been reduced to tears, and she'd pleaded for Raven's forgiveness and a fresh start. Brenda had been less effusive, but she'd accepted their decision to marry. He was confident their parents wouldn't interfere in their relationship going forward.

They'd entered their marriage with their parents' blessing and the past put to rest. Desmond, Esme and Kelvin were in jail awaiting trial. Jay's family had the comfort of knowing his murderers wouldn't walk free.

She twined her arms around his neck. "Have I told you lately how much I adore you?"

"No, you haven't. You're seriously slacking, wife."

"I adore you, Professor Ferrer."

"That's more like it."

She laughed, and he bent his head to capture

the delightful sound with his mouth. Moments passed as their world narrowed.

"We're really blessed, aren't we?" she said with a note of seriousness.

"We are."

"We have to count our blessings every day, even when you drink from the milk carton and forget to take out the trash."

"And when you store my socks and undershirts in the bathroom linen closet."

"What? It makes sense to me."

Aiden laughed. "You're my greatest blessing, Raven."

"And you're mine."

* * * * *

If you enjoyed this story, look for
these other books by Karen Kirst:

Targeted for Revenge
Smoky Mountain Ambush

Dear Reader,

I hope you enjoyed this third story featuring mounted police heroes. I was inspired to write about a dyslexic heroine after my sons and I read a children's book about the subject in our home-school curriculum. It's interesting how our self-views impact our decisions. Although Raven is a capable, courageous woman, she has unresolved issues lingering from childhood. She enters into a relationship with Aiden with deep reservations, and they eventually spill out and threaten to destroy their future. I'm happy they found their way back to each other, aren't you?

If you'd like to learn more about the Smoky Mountain Defender series and other books, check out my website at www.karenkirst.com. You can also sign up for my monthly newsletter. I'm active on Facebook, or you can email me at karenkirst@live.com.

Blessings,
Karen Kirst

Get 4 FREE REWARDS!

We'll send you 2 FREE Books plus 2 FREE Mystery Gifts.

FREE
Value Over
$20

Both the **Love Inspired®** and **Love Inspired® Suspense** series feature compelling novels filled with inspirational romance, faith, forgiveness, and hope.